Double-click into this sensational collection and read about Dean and Jamie who hacked into the government's most secret files – by accident; or Brian who swapped his brain with his computer; and the girl whose dad built her the most intelligent robot ever. Discover Sebastian, rescued from imprisonment in a computer game, and join Surfer, Qwerty and Rom in their virtually real world.

These brilliant stories by top modern authors like Malorie Blackman and Helen Dunmore are so exciting that you won't want to go back to your computer!

SENSATIONAL CYBER STORIES

COLLECTED BY
TONY BRADMAN

CORGI BOOKS

A CORGI BOOK : 0 552 54525 2

First published in Great Britain by Doubleday,
a division of Transworld Publishers Ltd

PRINTING HISTORY
Doubleday edition published 1997
Corgi edition published 1998

Set in Bembo by
Phoenix Typesetting, Ilkley, West Yorkshire.

Corgi Books are published by Transworld Publishers Ltd,
61–63 Uxbridge Road, Ealing, London W5 5SA,
in Australia by Transworld Publishers (Australia) Pty. Ltd,
15–25 Helles Avenue, Moorebank, NSW 2170,
and in New Zealand by Transworld Publishers (NZ) Ltd,
3 William Pickering Drive, Albany, Auckland.

Printed and bound in Great Britain by
Mackays of Chatham PLC, Chatham, Kent.

CONTENTS

PROJECT NEMESIS

by Tony Bradman

'And another thing, Dean,' said Dad, tapping the steering wheel as he glowered through the windscreen. The car in front hadn't budged for the last ten minutes. 'You were very late going to sleep last night. It was past twelve when I came in, and I'm pretty sure I heard your computer.'

'You couldn't have, Dad,' said Dean, hurriedly. He had switched it off and dived under his duvet the instant he'd heard Dad's feet on the stairs. 'I was in bed *long* before ten o'clock. Honest, I swear.'

Dad sighed, and turned to face him. Dean realized they had reached the stage of his father's lectures when Dad would start talking in his 'let's-be-grown-up-about-this' tone of voice. Now it was Dean's turn to glower through the windscreen, and silently pray for the traffic to un–jam.

'Look, Dean,' said Dad. 'We both know you were playing one of those dreadful games. You never seem to do anything else at the moment. Don't you get tired of blowing people apart and splattering brains everywhere?'

'Computer games aren't all like that, Dad,' said Dean, offended. Why was it adults always thought the worst of the stuff kids enjoyed? 'I don't just play shoot-'em-ups, anyway. They're OK, but I like strategy games best. *Sim City, World Domination, Megabyte War . . .*'

'That's all very well,' said Dad. 'But your mother and I just wish you'd spend a bit more time doing your homework, and a bit less playing computer games. They can't possibly be doing you any good, can they?'

Dean fumed inside. What did Dad know about it? Dad had never actually played a computer game in his life, so he had no idea how difficult some of them could be. They were much more demanding than most homework. You needed a whole range of skills to play them.

Not that there was any point telling Dad that. He simply wouldn't believe it. As far as Dad was concerned, they were *games*, and games meant *fun*, which you obviously weren't supposed to have. Ever.

'I'll try, Dad,' said Dean, arranging his face in that especially sincere expression he reserved for use during a Dad lecture. Total surrender was usually the only means of bringing the agony to an end.

'I'm glad to hear it,' said Dad, and Dean relaxed, sensing that this morning's Bore-A-Thon was probably over. It hadn't really been that bad, either, he thought. About four point five on the Dad Drone-O-Meter.

Dean had been expecting a nine, at least. Dad had been very grumpy all week. There seemed to be some sort of crisis at the office, and Dad had been getting home later and later every night. This morning Dean had heard him telling Mum he would have to work through the weekend.

Mum had not been pleased. And Mum could be a holy terror when she was cross. Dean was relieved he'd be spending *his* weekend sleeping over at his best friend's place. He was going straight to Jamie's house with him immediately after school finished.

'I think the traffic's about to move, Dad,' said Dean, peering up the road over the stationary cars. The lights had changed from red to green.

'Is it?' muttered Dad, his eyes snapping to the car in front. Dean noticed an edge of desperation in his voice. 'You're right, thank goodness. I should have been at the office ages ago. Put the radio on, will you?'

Dean reached forward and pressed the FM switch.

'. . . *continued major traffic jams throughout the Greater Metropolitan area this Friday a.m.,*' an announcer was saying. *'Reports are also coming in of a series of bizarre incidents involving the emergency services . . .'*

'Oh no!' groaned Dad. Dean glanced at his father. Dad was listening to the radio as if his life depended on it. His whole attention was focused on the announcer's words. Dean was puzzled. Why should Dad be so worried by a news story about police cars and fire ambulances turning up at the city's TV studios for no apparent reason? Dean shrugged.

He would never understand grown-ups.

'You can let me out if you like, Dad,' he said. 'It's only ten minutes' walk from here, and the lights have changed again.' Dad's shoulders slumped.

'You don't want me to be late for school, do you?'

'Certainly not,' said Dad, pulling sharply to a halt at the kerb. There was an angry honk from the car behind. Dean opened the door, and heard sirens wailing in the distance. 'Bye, son,' said Dad as Dean got out. Dean had hardly shut the door before Dad pulled back into the line of cars.

He was still stuck in the same place when Dean turned the corner.

'Are you sure we can get away with this, Jamie?' whispered Dean. He shifted uncomfortably on the swivel chair and glanced at his friend. It was late that Friday evening, and the two boys were sitting side by side at Jamie's desk. 'I mean, my dad will kill me if he finds out.'

'You worry too much,' said Jamie, his eyes focused on the glowing computer screen in front of them. 'He's not going to find out. We'll just log on, have a look around, then vanish like a pair of cyber-ghosts. OK?'

No, it wasn't OK, Dean thought uneasily, but he didn't say anything. He knew there was simply no stopping his friend once he'd picked up the scent of a new site he could hack into. Jamie thought he was the High Priest of Teen Hackers, a super-duper Net snooper from way back.

Things had been fine until Dean had let slip he knew the password Dad used to access his office computer. Dad was always forgetting it, so he kept it written on the pad by the phone. Jamie's ears had pricked up, and it hadn't taken him long to extract the password from Dean.

From that moment on, Jamie just couldn't wait for his mum and dad to go to bed. He hadn't even wanted to sneak down and watch the late, late horror movie on cable. He'd had one activity on his mind, and one alone. And that was hacking into Dean's dad's office computer.

Dean had done a little light hacking with Jamie before, and their usual targets were relatively risk-free. They *had* penetrated the school records database a couple of times, but the most exciting piece of information they'd uncovered there was the Head's middle name.

Dean's dad, however, worked for an organization that was rather more important, and potentially more dangerous for hackers – the government.

'Hey, we're in!' said Jamie triumphantly. Dean's heart sank. A list of government departments was swiftly scrolling up the screen. 'What exactly does your dad do?' asked Jamie, his fingers still clicking on keys.

'How should I know?' said Dean.

'You're a great help, aren't you?' said Jamie. 'Right, I think we'll try . . . *this* one,' he said, and clicked firmly on a large, shield-shaped icon with a lightning flash and the words *Central Security* emblazoned on it.

Password and coding questions filled the screen one after the other. Jamie started trying to field them, but Dean could see his friend was struggling. Dean felt his reluctance giving way to curiosity, and the urge to face the challenge this distant computer was throwing at them.

It was no contest for them together. Twenty minutes later, Dean and Jamie were browsing through some files with impressive titles. *Buildings Security, Personnel, Links to Intelligence Agencies.* That one was even marked *Top Secret* . . . Dean started to feel uncomfortable again.

'Wow!' said Jamie. 'That is *so* cool!' A small, simple

window had appeared. Inside it was a single word –
Nemesis – and the image of a grinning, silver and black
death's head. 'I just *have* to see what it is,' said Jamie,
and clicked on the icon before Dean could stop him.

'Er . . . Jamie,' he said. 'I have a bad feeling about
this.'

'Relax,' said Jamie, his fingers flashing. 'We're on a
roll now, old buddy. Besides, what could possibly
happen? They'll never find us.'

Suddenly the window in the screen vanished, and a
new one appeared. Inside it were a lot more words.
'*Warning! System accessed by unauthorized terminal. On-line
search initiated . . . proceeding . . .*'

'Oh no,' muttered Dean, watching in horror as the
word '*proceeding*' blinked in the corner of the window.
'Do something, Jamie!'

'I don't have to, Dean,' said Jamie, leaning back
smugly. 'I've seen this kind of stuff before. It's like the
X-Files Web site. You log on, and a warning comes up
saying the FBI is on its way to arrest you. It's a joke.'

'I'm not laughing,' said Dean. 'And I'd be a lot
happier if we logged off this particular site . . . *right now*.
I don't know about you, but I have plans for my life,
and they don't include spending a large chunk of it in
prison.'

'OK, OK,' said Jamie with a sigh. 'If you're going to
be a wimp.'

Jamie clicked on the window – but couldn't get it to

close. He clicked again, and again, his brow furrowed, and still nothing happened.

Then the word '*proceeding*' was replaced by . . . '*TRACED*'.

'Just turn it off, Jamie,' said Dean, his voice rising in panic.

Jamie didn't have to be told twice. He reached past Dean and jabbed the off switch on the modem connecting the computer to the Internet. The *Nemesis* window folded in on itself and the screen went dark.

Both boys let out a sigh, and turned to look at each other.

'I'll bet it was a trick to put hackers off,' said Jamie with a nervous laugh. Dean knew he was trying to convince himself as much as anyone.

'You're probably right,' said Dean, and Jamie smiled.

But later, as Dean lay stiffly in his sleeping-bag on Jamie's bedroom floor, he couldn't get a particular image out of his mind. And that silver and black death's head pursued him relentlessly through his dreams . . .

Dean was in a locked room, cowering in the corner, and somebody — or *something* — was pounding at the door, trying to smash through it and get him. Then he realized he was dreaming, and opened his eyes.

But the pounding continued.

Somebody *was* hammering at the front door of the

house, and there were plenty of other noises, too – loud voices, running feet, a whooshing, beating sound that seemed to be coming from above the roof.

'Wow, a *chopper*,' shouted Jamie. Dean sat up, and saw his friend kneeling on the bed. He was looking out of the window. '*A-mazing*.'

'What's going on?' Dean yelled.

'No idea, pal,' Jamie shouted happily. 'But I have a feeling we might well be in a little trouble. I *don't* believe it. I've just seen a guy with a *gun* out there! Hey, it's a whole SWAT team, and they're all over the garden!'

Dean groaned and burrowed deep into his sleeping-bag.

But there was no escape. He heard Jamie's dad stomp down and open the front door, followed by Jamie's mum. There was a shouted conversation in the hall with somebody outside. It sounded quite heated.

At last, several pairs of feet thumped up the stairs, and the bedroom door was opened. Jamie's dad put his head round, and spoke.

'You two had better come downstairs,' he said, grimly. Dean caught a glimpse of helmets behind him on the landing. Each one bore a distinctive symbol – a shield containing a lightning flash and the letters CS . . .

A few moments later, Dean and Jamie were sitting on the sofa in the front room. Jamie's dad was sitting in one

armchair, and his mum in another. Dean could tell that both of them were pretty angry.

There wasn't much they could do, though. An armed SWAT team-member was standing by the door. Another armed man with three stripes on his dark-uniformed arm was speaking quietly into a radio head-set.

'Central from Alpha Squad,' he said. 'Location secured, over.' Then he turned to Jamie's mum and dad. 'Someone will be arriving soon who will be able to answer your questions. If you could remain patient . . .'

'Cool,' whispered Jamie, nudging Dean. 'It's just like the scene in *Final Strike III* when the rogue SWAT team wipe out that family . . .' Jamie noticed his dad glaring at him. 'Er . . . sorry, Dad,' he said, and shut up.

'This is outrageous,' said Jamie's mum. 'How dare you barge into my house with some wild story about national security. I won't . . .'

She didn't get a chance to finish. Just then, two more people entered the room. Dean glanced up, and swallowed hard. One was a tired-looking man with staring eyes. He was carrying a shiny, aluminium brief-case.

The other was Dean's dad.

'Thank you, Sergeant,' Dad said to the man with the head-set. 'I'll take over from here. You and your men can get back to base.'

The sergeant saluted, and slipped out with his fellow

SWAT team-member. Once the door was closed behind them, Jamie's mum and dad leaped to their feet and started shouting at Dean's dad. Then Jamie's dad suddenly stopped, and peered more closely at the man in front of him.

'Hang on,' he said, suspiciously. 'But you're Dean's dad, aren't you? I think we've met before, haven't we? At the school open evening? Don't tell me, this is all a set-up for one of those funny TV programmes, isn't it?' He grinned at his wife. 'I'll bet there's a hidden camera somewhere.'

'I'm afraid there isn't,' said Dean's dad. 'What's happening is very real. Now, if you'll just sit down, I'll try and explain everything to you as quickly as I can. Then I have something to ask these two.'

'It's OK, Dad,' said Dean, gloomily. 'I confess. Jamie and me hacked into your office computer. But we could never have done it if I hadn't supplied the password. It's all my fault, really. I'm sorry.'

'I'm glad to hear it,' said Dad with a wry smile. 'But I already knew you were the culprits, actually, and I had another question in mind. How would you boys like to *help* us — the government, that is?'

For a second Dean wondered if he was still dreaming after all.

'It sounds like an absolute *nightmare*,' Jamie's mum was saying, taking a mug of tea and a biscuit from the tray

Jamie's dad had just brought in. 'Although I'm not quite sure I understand everything you've told us.'

'Come on, Mum,' said Jamie, rolling his eyes at Dean. 'It's dead simple. The government developed some fancy new software designed to unite all official computers into one big system. They installed it last month, there was a bug in it, and it's gone wrong. Like HAL in *2001*, or the big computer in *The Terminator* and *Terminator 2*.'

'That's right,' said Dean's dad. 'In fact, the system is responding in an extreme way, almost as if it's being threatened. When a traffic control video camera records someone going through an amber light, the system picks it up and instantly changes every light in the city to red.'

'Oh, I *see*,' said Jamie's mum. 'Now we know why the traffic was so awful everywhere this morning. And you say things are getting worse?'

Dean listened, fascinated. Part of the system monitored TV broadcasts, and was ordering police and ambulances to the studios every time anyone seemed to be hurt in films or cartoons. Another part had sent the Defence Secretary to a bunker to protect him three days ago, then locked him in.

Yet another had sent out a full SWAT team when Dean and Jamie's hacking was traced, although in fact they'd been lucky. The system had ordered a tactical air-strike when some adult hackers had been detected. Only a frantic, last-minute phone call to the air-base had saved them.

Dad said he'd been given the task of co-ordinating the attempt to deal with the crisis. But like most of the senior people working for the government, he knew nothing about computers. So they had called on some experts, a team led by the man who had come with Dad.

His name was Professor Lloyd, and he had been working round the clock. No wonder he seemed exhausted.

Dad was looking pretty tired, too, thought Dean.

'OK, I think we're clear on all that now,' said Jamie's dad. 'But what *I* still don't understand is how Jamie and Dean can help you.'

'Over to you, Professor,' said Dad. 'That's *your* department.'

'Well, it's quite straightforward, really, if a little embarrassing,' said the computer expert, and smiled, nervously. 'As soon as the first problems occurred, we installed a radical clean-up program – *Project Nemesis*. But the system closed it down, and no-one has been able to get to it since.'

Dean and Jamie looked at each other.

'We did,' they said, in unison.

'Exactly!' said Professor Lloyd, excited. 'We can still monitor some of what's happening in the system, so we knew you'd hacked in. We checked your response times, and they're incredible! Better than any of the . . .

adults in my team. We believe you're the only people who can reactivate *Nemesis* and debug the system before there's a major catastrophe.'

'But we only saw the icon,' said Dean. 'We didn't have time to get into the program before this other window flashed up and cut us off.'

'Ah, that was probably because the terminal you were working with wasn't powerful enough,' said Professor Lloyd. 'We're certain that if you had something a little more beefy . . .' he said, opening the aluminium brief-case and displaying its contents, '. . . you'd get a lot further.'

'Whoa!' said Jamie, awe-struck. 'That's a top-of-the-range THX 1138!'

'You *do* know your computers, don't you?' said Professor Lloyd, impressed. 'So, do you two think you can handle this little baby? We can just plug it straight into your normal modem, and away you go.'

'*Can* we?' said Jamie. 'Watch us! It'll be a doddle, won't it, Dean?'

'Yeah, I suppose so,' said Dean. Then he paused, and looked at his father. 'But I have the feeling something is missing here, Dad. What happened to all that stuff about how bad playing computer games is for me? Or does this prove they can do kids good as well?'

'OK, you win,' said Dad. 'I agree, they've obviously done *something* to your fevered brain, and I'm grudgingly prepared to admit the effect might even be good.

21

I'm certainly hoping it will come in useful as far as saving the world is concerned. And I don't mean to hurry you, but . . .'

'One last question, Dad,' said Dean, smiling. 'Seeing as Jamie and me *are* about to save the world, is there any chance we might be in line for some kind of . . . well, reward? You know, something like large amounts of money, new computers, hundreds of new computer games?'

'How about total immunity from criminal prosecution for illegal hacking?' said Dad, smiling back. 'And if you're really lucky, I might even provide some support when you tell your mother what you've been up to. Somehow I don't think she's going to be too happy with you.'

'Er . . . OK, Dad,' said Dean, hurriedly. 'It's a deal. Right, Jamie. Time we got upstairs and started kicking some computer butt. Coming, Dad? You never know, if you pay attention, you might even learn something.'

'Oh, I doubt that, Dean,' said Dad with a smile. 'I doubt that very much.'

But father and son went out of the room together.

SURFER AND THE DREAMCASTLE

by Steve Bowkett

The VR-Bar was quiet this evening, most of the after-workers and kids on-trek from school having left. Only the real Cybernet phreaks – the Web Heads – had stayed behind. They were all on-line in their groups, deep into whatever dataspace adventure they had chosen.

Surfer, Qwerty and Rom had zoned-in to *The Dreamcastle* again. It was their favourite virtual Web site, and they'd been visiting this part of it for the past six months . . .

The Dreamcastle, an interactive game-zone that was a cross between the Minotaur's labyrinth, a pyramid temple to the great god Ra, and Dracula's Transylvanian mountain-top mansion. The dialogue box that popped up in front of your eyes like a spinning crystal at the outset said that the Castle was twenty kilometres wide, fifteen broad, five high, and had a thousand levels – each one containing greater dangers and excitements than the one below.

'Well, this is it. The big day – level five hundred.'

Surfer grinned, unable to keep the pride off his face. The three of them had worked hard, and as a team, to enable this to happen. Qwerty wished she had Surfer's confidence. Since early summer they had come here together, battling against cyber knights, digital dragons, demons made out of fire and smoke, the usual rather boring versions of Frankenstein's monster, the Mummy and Wolfman, vampires that looked like friendly salesmen in grey suits – and a hundred other opponents that, of course, they always managed to defeat.

'Now it gets harder,' Qwerty pointed out, wanting to wipe the cocky smile off her friend's face. 'Now the Castle does all it can to stop us going any higher.'

'It'll be no problem,' Surfer declared. He clapped a hand on Rom's shoulder. 'With Rom's knowledge of Web site short cuts, with my brains and your experience of similar games, Qwerty, we'll reach level one thousand inside a year!'

'The only way is up,' Qwerty muttered, letting Surfer have his day.

'On-line!' the kids chorused, which was the password for dropping into the virtual reality world of the game . . .

Outside the VR–Bar, beyond the garish gleam of its

neon, October rain was falling and the twilight streets were shiny wet. But in *The Dreamcastle*, Surfer and the others found themselves standing on a stone balcony, two kilometres high, looking out over sunny summer countryside.

Surfer, fourteen years old, tall and self-assured, went right to the edge – and felt his feet tingling at the huge distance dropping away to a miniature landscape of rocky slopes, forest and a river valley far below. 'It's only a game,' he whispered to himself, to help dispel the fear. 'I'm not really here . . .'

He felt a cool wind buffeting his hair and rustling his heavy cloak around him. Rom, quiet and nervous, dared a peek and let out a soft moan of pure fear.

'I . . . I have never been so high . . .'

Surfer grinned, taking hold of Rom's elbow to steady him.

'Isn't it just ace!' He breathed in the wind and the sun and the sheer pleasure of being alive—

Then, without warning, the sun was gone as a tumble of black cloud spilled out over the highest peaks of the Castle, rolling thunder before it and cracking the sky like blue porcelain with jagged white lightning.

Rom squealed like a redcap elf and jumped back. Qwerty had time to look up in amazement at the winged serpent plummeting out of the storm.

It was big, it was mean, its tongue flickered like fire and its scaly sides were the colour of chrome. Black talons flicked out and hooked themselves to pluck Surfer off the ledge.

He was ready, sword in hand, because the Dreamcastle was always at its most dangerous when it seemed at its most peaceful.

As the storm-dragon dropped, Surfer swung the blade. Astonishingly, he thought, he missed the monster completely, cutting empty air. Qwerty had been right: after level 500, things got *much* more difficult.

The next second the storm-dragon's claws had snagged his cloak and he was whirled up into the sky.

The monster shrieked in triumph and lowered its head to devour him. Surfer was having none of it. As the awful mouth loomed close, he drew back his arm and drove the weapon deep into the foul hot throat of the creature.

It gushed screams and much blood, suddenly losing its balance in the sky and tumbling downwards out of control.

Surfer saw the ground whipping round and round, the Castle walls blurring past him. He knew he had seconds left before the dying storm-dragon crushed him against the stonework, or – moments later – crashed with him into the forest.

He took a gamble, knowing failure could risk his high score in this phase of the game. Disentangling himself from the beast's claws, he unclipped his cloak, picked his moment – then swung himself in towards the wall.

Surfer's shoulder hit rock and the pain flared through him. His sword fell from a numbed hand, spinning away out of sight. With his other hand, he grabbed a mass of clinging ivy; it whipped through his fingers, stripping off skin, but gradually slowed him until he hung there, breathless, gazing down at the dwindling shape of the storm-dragon smashing into the trees.

The thunder and lightning – created by the dragon as camouflage – quickly faded with the death of the beast into a mist of pixels. The sun came out and created the illusion of warming Surfer's back as he scrambled down the ivy and slid through the nearest glassless window —

— into a dim chamber that smelled of damp straw and misery.

Chains tinkled in the shadows. Something moved.

Surfer pressed himself back against the wall, his left hand drawing a knife from its belt-sheath, as his eyes adjusted to the darkness.

'Please . . .' came a small, frightened voice. 'Please help me . . .'

Squinting hard, Surfer began to make out the slim, huddled shape of a girl. She was about his own age, pale-skinned, her long fair hair matted with straw, her ankle-length dress grimy and ripped to tatters.

She lifted a hand towards him and chains clinked again. The girl was manacled to the wall, obviously afraid, desperately needing his help.

'Stay calm,' Surfer said, stepping towards her. 'I'll take a look at those chains—'

'Hurry!' Her voice was suddenly urgent. 'If *he* comes and catches you here, he'll destroy you!'

'Who?'

'Tsepesh,' the girl told him, her voice trembling. 'Tsepesh the Sorcerer, Lord of the Dreamcastle and the Vale of Nightmare . . .'

Surfer had heard of him, this Darklord, who dwelt, not in the Castle's high towers, but deep in the basements and cellars with the worms, with the unseen crawling things. Tsepesh was one of the Major Fiends inhabiting this level of the game.

'Don't worry about it now – and hold still,' Surfer said, grasping the girl's thin cold hand as he examined the locks on her wrists.

He had time to think that the VR software's creation of the girl's hand was not entirely convincing, before something boomed deep in the heart of the Dreamcastle, and footsteps clumped distantly on stone floors – but drawing closer.

'He's coming—' The girl's body began to shake in her terror. And Surfer, without his sword, without his friends, felt helpless.

'I'll come back for you, I promise . . . Tell me your name,' he asked.

She smiled, almost coyly. 'It's Annabelle.'

Not far away, an iron door screamed on its hinges.

There came a grunting sound, as of a big animal smelling a stranger.

'I'll come back for you,' Surfer repeated. He made the circular motion with his hands that called the dialogue box into existence. It was voice controlled, and all he had to do now was say the word 'off-line' to end the game . . .

But his eyes lingered a little longer on Annabelle's slight form, and there was a tightness of longing in his chest that he'd never known before.

The air grew sharp with the stink of burning metal. Nails scraped on stone. The breathing of Tsepesh the Darklord sounded like a smithy's bellows.

'Who are you?' Annabelle wondered.

'Call me Surfer,' he said, the word sounding strange on his lips. He spoke the rune of ending. 'Off-line!'

There was a flash of light and a rainbow spiral of colours.

With a jolt, Surfer found himself back in the VR-Bar, the datasuit feeling tight and uncomfortable around him.

Rom helped him take off the kit, while Qwerty efficiently logged their progress in the game, noting Surfer had reached a high score in his defeat of the storm-dragon.

'What the heck happened to you in there?' Qwerty wanted to know. She had always been the nosiest member of the group.

Surfer shook his head and smiled wistfully. It still seemed all too ridiculous.

'I'll tell you over a coffee,' he said. 'But whatever happens, I've got to get back in there – and quickly.'

'You realize she's only an NPC,' Rom pointed out as they finished coffee and a big plateful of chocolate doughnuts. Surfer licked his fingers free of chocolate, then wiped them with a napkin. He grinned.

'But she was so *real* . . .'

He knew, of course, that Rom was only guessing that Annabelle was an NPC – a Non-Player Character created inside the mind of the computer.

'I mean, she was so beautiful.'

Qwerty chuckled. She was fifteen, tall and raven-haired, self-assured and very pretty. 'That's just typical of boys! You'll do anything for a girl with a nice face and a sad note in her voice . . . But don't you realize that the computer is trying to trick you? How do you know that Annabelle isn't on the side of Tsepesh . . . ? Maybe she's his daughter . . . His wife even!'

Surfer made a sneering sound, but Rom was looking serious as he interrupted. 'It's worth listening to Qwerty. She's been surfing the Net since she was eight years old. She's seen some things – she's met some enemies. You said as much yourself.'

'OK!' Surfer threw up his hands to put an end to the arguments. 'Maybe – just maybe – Annabelle doesn't really exist. But you know as well as I do that it's very hard to check. You'd need to do some pretty serious hacking to break into the program to find out . . .'

Rom shrugged his shoulders and smiled innocently. 'I can do it,' he said brightly. 'Give me a couple of hours and I can tell if she's a real girl, or just a ghost in the machine.'

An unexpected anger flared in Surfer's chest. Suddenly he felt that Rom and Qwerty were trying to make him seem stupid and small.

Surfer stood up, jabbing a finger in Rom's direction.

'Well you just go ahead and do that, why don't you? But you know something – I don't care. Whatever you find out about Annabelle, I'm still going back in there tomorrow to rescue her.'

'But the Darklord, Tsepesh—' Rom began.

'He's very devious,' Qwerty added.

Surfer was already walking away.

'We reached level five hundred together . . . But now I see I don't need you any more. You're slowing me down. I'll destroy Tsepesh and save Annabelle by myself. All you've got to do, guys, is stay out of my way . . .'

They watched him walk across the lobby of the VR-Bar and out into the street. An autotaxi pulled up at Surfer's request, he stepped inside and it whisked him away.

Qwerty shook her head disapprovingly. 'He'll regret

it,' she said. '*The Dreamcastle* is the cleverest game there is . . . Why, some folks have spent years trying to defeat the Darklord and reach the top . . .'

'I worry about him.' Rom stirred his coffee and lifted the cup to his lips. 'So I think I will spend those couple of hours just checking out exactly who "Annabelle" really is . . .'

Surfer swiped his credit card through the reader in the back of the autotaxi, said goodnight to the robodriver and walked across the street to his house. His parents and sister, Sarah, were still up playing 3D Monopoly in the living room. Surfer called that he was home, then went straight up to his room and to bed . . .

His dreams that night were troubled, tangled up with the *Dreamcastle* adventure he'd played that day. Once again he was struggling with the storm-dragon in the sky, falling through the air, grabbing the clinging vines and scrambling into the little dungeon cell where Annabelle was kept prisoner . . .

'Help me . . .' she pleaded in that helpless, terrified voice. 'Help me . . .'

Surfer found himself battling with the manacles and chains, his efforts becoming more desperate as he heard the Darklord clumping along the stone corridor . . . Coming closer . . . Coming closer . . . Until finally the dungeon door started to swing open and a curl of red smoke drifted in through the opening.

At that point, Surfer lost his nerve. With a cry of fear he leaped away from Annabelle and fumbled at his hip for his sword. But, of course, the sword was missing, and a knife would never be enough to destroy the Lord of the Dreamcastle and the Vale of Nightmare . . .

So he turned with a wail of despair for the window – Annabelle's scream behind him, and then the white heat of Tsepesh's talons raking down his back—

Surfer woke with a cry, sitting up in bed. He was covered with sweat and felt very confused, so that, just for a second or two, Annabelle's voice echoed in his room, and the smell of damp straw and misery lingered in his nostrils, and her face floated in the blackness, imploring him to save her.

Surfer reckoned he knew a lot about *The Dreamcastle*: it was a VR game he'd played regularly for years. Kids would come up to him at school and ask his advice; they admired him for all the battles he'd won, all the foes he'd defeated. From being a nobody, just another Web Head who liked to surf the Net, he'd become recognized as an authority and a hero, one of the few who'd made it this far.

And yet, although he'd heard plenty about Tsepesh the Darklord, he'd never seen him. Nobody ever did, until they got to level 501. From then on, you saw more and more of him, until his true and awful face was revealed.

Thinking about this, Surfer wondered if it wouldn't be better to try and rescue Annabelle without battling against Tsepesh . . . Any foolhardy swashbuckling swordsman could puff out his chest and go rushing stupidly into battle. But the Darklord had enchantments beyond imagining, clever deceits and tricks he would use to confuse you. He could conjure up your most terrifying nightmare and send it howling into your face. For every weapon you might use against him, the Darklord had a hundred in return. Nobody he knew had beaten the monstrous Tsepesh, Surfer realized, smiling as he made his decision. Nobody had beaten him – *because everybody had tried to.*

So the way to rescue Annabelle was to do something that no game-playing cyber phreak had ever done before . . .

Rom and Qwerty spent their lunch hour next day at school in the Computer Block. Other kids were accessing encyclopaedias or being characters in virtual reality storybooks. But Rom hacked straight in to the VR-Bar's main miniCray computer and quickly located the root-files of *The Dreamcastle*'s software.

With Qwerty wearing a head-set beside him, Rom created a huge book hanging in space. Each page gave details of a character in the game. He zipped straight to 'Annabelle' – and found nothing.

'So,' Qwerty said, frowning, 'either she's a real girl . . .'

'Or she lied, and has another name,' Rom added. He gave Annabelle's description to the book and told it to *seek* . . . The pages began to turn by themselves, flickering faster and faster until they stopped abruptly at a main entry.

For a few moments, Rom didn't understand what was happening.

Then all the blood drained from his face.

'Qwerty – have you seen Surfer today?'

The girl looked flustered. 'Um – well – come to think of it—'

'The fool!' Rom yelled. 'I know what he's done . . . He's skipped school to go to the VR-Bar. He meant what he said to us yesterday. That idiot Surfer is going to try and rescue "Annabelle" by himself!'

Surfer had made his preparations carefully. Now he hung by a fine line, high above the forest canopy, dark-green ivy leaves hiding him from sight. A gentle wind brought the slightly chemical computerized smell of woodsmoke to his nostrils. He smiled, knowing he'd be down there soon, with Annabelle in his arms, having won the girl *and* the glory – and more importantly still, being the first to have outwitted the Darklord.

He unslung a pack from his back, clipped it firmly to

the stonework, and released the billowing green folds of his paraglider. Then, like a nimble spider, Surfer slid further down on the line, pushed against the wall, swung outwards, and in through the window space to Annabelle's gloomy cell.

'You came back!' she cried, standing as she saw him.

'I said I would . . . Now hold still!'

He drew some diamond wire from his belt-pouch, and began to saw through the black metal manacles. Far away, metal scraped on stone and some dreadful animal bellowed.

'It's him . . .' Her voice quivered.

The first manacle dropped away as the diamond wire sliced through it like butter.

'Your other hand!' Surfer said urgently.

Now he could hear the heavy pounding footsteps of Tsepesh coming down the corridor towards the cell. The beast howled, smelling the intruder.

'We won't make it!' Annabelle clung tightly to Surfer. He tutted, eased her away, and continued with his task.

Within a very few seconds, the second shackle fell free. Surfer grabbed Annabelle's hand and hurried her over to the window. He pushed her up on to the ledge.

'But we're miles high!'

'Grip the bar you see outside,' he commanded, 'and clip that strap around you.'

With a deafening shriek of metal, the dungeon door

exploded inwards. Black smoke and white flame swept through the room.

Annabelle screamed. Surfer snatched a glass globe from his pouch and hurled it down to shatter on the flagstones. As the special liquid came into contact with air, it flared up into a dazzling curtain of light.

The thing in the smoke screeched in agony, blinded by the brilliance. But Tsepesh was also angered beyond measure, and lunged out towards the mortal human boy who'd tried to trick him.

Surfer caught a glimpse of a vast clawed hand, the middle finger decorated with a ring of black iron. He whipped out his knife and threw it, spinning, to embed itself in the monster's flesh.

The Darklord's screams rose in pitch and became unbearable.

Surfer turned away, wrapped one arm around Annabelle's slim waist, and with the other released the paraglider's clamps, before snatching at the bar and launching them off into cyberspace.

'I'm so grateful,' Annabelle said, leaning forward to kiss Surfer tenderly on the cheek. 'I got myself into such difficulty playing *The Dreamcastle*. Every time I went into the game I ended up in that awful dungeon . . .'

'It could happen to anybody,' Surfer said with a shrug. He kept the smile of pride and triumph off his face this time. But he was greatly pleased, not only by the fact that he'd beaten the Darklord, but that Annabelle had turned out to be real . . . So much for Rom's fancy theory!

'Um, listen,' Surfer said, 'why don't I buy you a coffee? They do a great chocolate doughnut here too,' he suggested. Annabelle beamed, her whole face lighting up with delight.

'Sure, whatever you say . . . And thanks again . . . I can't believe how easily the Darklord fooled me!'

'Don't worry about it. You're safe now, Annabelle. Let's go for that coffee . . .'

Surfer put his arm around her as they walked across the lobby to the coffee shop.

Behind them, the air shimmered and Rom and Qwerty flickered into existence. For a second or two they were puzzled.

'Wait a minute – this can't be right – this can't be the VR-Bar . . .' Qwerty said.

Rom was looking around frantically. 'No, it's level five hundred and one – and there's Surfer. Wait – stop! Say the rune of ending, Surfer! Say it now!'

Surfer and Annabelle had reached the coffee-shop door. Surfer began to turn on hearing Rom shouting after him. His face began to register shock and anger that he'd made such a simple mistake – so flushed with success had he been, and so flattered by Annabelle's admiration, that he'd failed to come out of VR at the end of the game episode. A level one beginner wouldn't have been that stupid!

Qwerty and Rom's computer-generated forms yelled their warning as they tried to reach him. But Annabelle grabbed his arm and swung him through the doorway.

Surfer glimpsed the damp stone walls of the dungeon beyond. But it was too late. Annabelle closed the door behind them. And it was Qwerty who noticed that the suddenly huge middle finger was decorated with a plain black iron ring.

BRIAN AND THE BRAIN

by Sara Vogler and Janet Burchett

Brian had homework. It was writing, and writing was a bit of a problem for Brian. Whatever he produced, it would look as if a drunken spider had staggered across the page. Whatever he produced, he knew what Miss Spenshaw would say.

'It may be the best work in the history of the school, Brian, but as I can't read it we shall never know, shall we? Perhaps we could fax it off to Beijing for a translation.'

There's nothing like a good joke, thought Brian, and that's nothing like a good joke.

Of course, there would be no problem if he could do it on the computer. But last week, while he'd been trying to install *Attack of the Killer Klingfilms*, Mum's story *Ellie and the Elves Go Skipping* had somehow got deleted. She'd been about to send it off to her publisher. Brian felt it was unfair. Mum had claimed that it was his fault. But the whole family knew what the computer was like. An eccentric, cranky old thing. Second-hand from the eccentric cranky old woman down the road, 'The Brain' had come into the family like an intelligent but unreliable dog. You never knew if it was going to lick, bite or wee on the carpet. You touched it at your peril. Dad wouldn't go near it. Not since the mouse had given him an electric shock.

The Brain had no sense of humour. In the face of the most ridiculous spelling mistake it would merely add a solemn red line underneath. It ignored Brian's expertise at space games – even when he got top of the top ten. And sometimes it would announce unexpectedly that you had performed an illegal operation and the pro-gram would now be closed down, or else. Brian often wondered what it would do – send the computer police round? He thought about what they would look like. Would they knock politely or beat your door down?

But when The Brain swallowed Ellie, along with twenty-four of her elfin friends, Brian's mother had gently discouraged him from using it for a while.

'If you ever touch that machine again, I will person-ally come into your assembly and read *Ellie and the Elves Go to the Farm* – with sound effects.'

So Brian thought he would give technology a miss for a few days.

But this was serious. The homework had to be in tomorrow. Otherwise, Miss Spenshaw had said, he could do it during football practice. Luckily, Mum was out in the garden having a fight with the ivy. She'd be ages. The ivy always won in the end. There was plenty of time to finish a game of *Space Bowls* and thrash out the homework too.

But first he had to put the wet sponges in Grace's bed and stick the plastic spider on her mirror. It was nearly a week since he'd glued her shoes to the bedroom floor. He mustn't let standards slip. When he got back to the computer he felt that a quick game of *Space Bowls* would loosen up his fingers nicely. He made level thirty-seven before being blown to pieces. Not bad. Now for the essay. Or should he have a quick game of *Giant Aphids of Andromeda?* No, he must be strong. He resigned himself to the unpleasant task ahead.

'All About Me'. How stupid. It was like being five again. Why couldn't Miss Spenshaw let him write about 'How to be world champion at *Marauding Martians*'? Or, 'My Hundred Best Practical Jokes'? He sighed, slumped down in his seat and typed:

all abot me bye Brain Bossley
PlEase see work done 6 weeks ago when
yooooooooou were off with the chicken
pox and WE HaD thAt naFF SUPPLy
teacher who kept falling aSleep.

```
zzzzzzzzzzzzzzz. i haven't cHanGEd
snincE then. i thank you.
```

He looked up and read what he'd written. Keyboard skills were not his strong point but at least she'd be able to read it. The Brain had put red lines under nearly every word. Brian ignored them. He didn't need keyboard skills, not when he was so ace with the mouse and the joystick. Then he remembered. He had to finish with 'My Greatest Wish'. He'd make them all laugh. He thought he might wish to be Mike Megabyte, hero of Alien Bashers Anon. He stared at the screen. He noticed he'd spelt his name wrong – Brain. That was it! Never mind Mike Megabyte, he'd have the lot. He'd have the entire brain of the computer. He'd reach level 1027 of *Thundering Terrapins* before they knew what had hit them. He wouldn't have to struggle with his hand-writing. He might even find maths easier if he could understand it. And he'd probably make even quicker quips. Yes, he'd have them rolling in the aisles. He'd probably get into *The Guinness Book of Records* – the Boy with a Brain the Size of Jupiter. But that sort of thing only happened in *Nova-nerds from Neptune* where you picked up extra brain-power as you went along. Slipping further down in his seat, he carried on typing.

```
i wish to swOp brains with my
cOmpouter.
```

He grabbed the mouse to click on 'print'. But the moment he did so he felt a weird sensation in his head. It was as if someone had flushed his brain. He could feel it emptying like a toilet cistern. Then, an army of electronic ants seemed to march from the mouse, into his fingers, up his arm and finally into his skull.

The back door banged.

'What are you up to, Brian?' shouted Mum. 'I hope you're not on that computer.'

Brian mechanically tidied up the computer table, tucked in the chair and marched up to bed without a word.

Next morning, Mum came in to give Brian the first of his time checks and increasingly unpleasant threats. She pulled back the curtains.

'Welcome to Windows,' said a loud voice behind her. She swung round. Brian was standing, fully dressed, beside an immaculately made bed. Mum couldn't believe it. She staggered out. Brian, feeling rather odd, marched down to breakfast behind her.

He stared at his cereal.

'There are two hundred and fifty-six Corn Crunchies in my bowl. The square root of two hundred and fifty-six is sixteen. Therefore it will only take me sixteen spoonfuls of sixteen Corn Crunchies to finish my cereal – with no remainder.'

'That was impressive, Brian,' said Dad when he'd

checked the arithmetic on the back of an envelope. He looked at his son. 'Are you OK, Brian? You're looking a bit pale.'

Brian considered this. He certainly did feel different this morning. And more surprisingly still, he found he wasn't interested in retrieving the spider and sponges before Grace threw them away. That all seemed rather childish and totally irrelevant now. But then, of course, when you had 1.6 gigabytes and 100 megahertz who needed jokes and space games? Maths, data, memory – that was the real world.

'Brian can't even add up,' said his sister grumpily. She'd had a bad night. 'He's got a brain the size of a Ricicle. He must've got it off the back of the cereal packet. I'm fed up with Corn Crunchies, Mum. Haven't we got anything else?'

'Did you know,' Brian piped up to his own surprise, 'just one click brings down a menu?'

His family ignored him. They were used to his jokes.

'One of these days,' Mum was saying to anyone who would listen, 'I'm going wallpaper shopping. I'm fed up with these spots. If I don't watch out, I'm going to find myself counting them . . .'

'There are two million, one hundred and sixty thousand, three hundred and thirty-seven spots on the kitchen walls,' announced Brian. Mum put her hand on his forehead.

'Are you feeling all right, Brian?' she asked.

'Everything is in normal view, thank you,' said Brian. 'And please call me Brain.'

He marched off to school.

Brian sat at his table. He laid out his pens, rulers and rubbers in neat rows. He finally managed to find his books in the clutter of his drawer, and arranged them symmetrically in front of him. Now he had customized his desktop he looked up – ready and waiting to impress.

'Brian Bossley,' said Miss Spenshaw sternly, 'if it's not too much to ask, could I have your homework please?'

'The file cannot be found,' said Brian, staring squarely at her. 'Please check that the correct file name has been entered.'

The class began to titter. Brian, the school clown, never failed. And more impressive, Brian was keeping a straight face.

'That's enough, Brian,' said Miss Spenshaw. 'I want to see "All About Me" – NOW!'

'Correct file name has been entered,' replied Brian. 'Ready to print. And please call me Brain.'

The class giggled. But for some reason Brian didn't look round with his usual merry grin. Miss Spenshaw stared. She hadn't expected him to do as he was told. Brian hadn't expected to do as he was told either. But he had to – she had issued a command.

He took a clean sheet of paper and carefully

sharpened a pencil. He did a mental spell check, sorted out the capital letters and completed a word count. He wondered why he had written this rubbish. It was pathetic for a boy with a brain the size of Jupiter.

'File name "All About Me" . . . font – extremely untidy . . . double space . . . font size – overlarge, twenty-six.'

With the speed of a printer, his work appeared on the paper. Only the ending had changed:

'Computers have no need for wishes, only commands. Tip of the day – did you know you can speed up your working efficiency with extra megabytes?'

With that, Brian suddenly got up and walked round the classroom collecting all the books. He put them into brown folders.

'What are you doing?' asked Miss Spenshaw.

'All work has now been saved in files,' announced Brian. The class started laughing.

'Good old Brian,' said Luke. 'He never fails.'

Brian felt a surge of irritation.

'Please call me Brain,' he snapped.

Meanwhile at home, Mum switched on the computer to do some work. The machine made a dreadful grinding noise.

'Wotcha!' read the screen.

Mum was surprised. Brian must have learnt how to customize the screen saver at last.

'Beep!'

The whole class jumped. Brian didn't usually go in for beeping.

'To gracebossley from williamwigeon@Stevenage BirdSanctuaryCo.UK. Spoonbills safely hatched. Mother and chicks doing well,' Brian announced.

Everyone fell about. Gradually the laughter died down as the kids realized that Brian wasn't joking. Brian ignored them and carried on with his maths.

'Brian . . . Brian!'

'Ready, Miss Spenshaw.'

'Thank you for sharing that with us, Brian. Perhaps you will kindly explain yourself.'

'Just delivering an e-mail message. And please call me Brain.'

Miss Spenshaw walked over and peered at Brian's work. Her jaw dropped down to her knees. Although it was as untidy as ever, it was all correct and he was on page twenty-two already.

Mum wasn't getting much work done. Ellie and the Elves hadn't finished packing their picnic basket yet. She had hoped to get them to the woods before lunch. She kept being interrupted by prompt boxes:

49

? What's for tea ?

and

! This story is soooooo bor-ing !

and

? Have you heard the one about the rabbit and the spirit level ?

The computer had even called her Mum twice and claimed it was too tired to do any work. Mum wished she had gone wallpaper shopping instead.

At break-time, Luke skidded up to Brian, hands out ready for the usual joystick wrist-actions and synchronized air-mousing. But Brian ignored him. He'd only been out there for three minutes and forty-eight point nine seconds and he'd already been pestered six times by children asking him to tell them jokes. No-one wanted Encarta. No-one needed a bar chart. No-one even asked after his database. He wanted to fulfil commands, save, edit, insert and take messages. He wanted to show them what he could do.

'Beep! To mrjohnbossley from robbie.reliant@ dodgymotors.Co.UK. Ford Capri E reg. Excellent condition. Egg yellow with green doors . . .'

'You're no fun any more, Brian Bossley,' said Luke. 'Your jokes are awful – and you've turned into a boffin.'

Brian considered the matter.

'Boffin. Not found in thesaurus. Suggest change to bodkin or bog.'

'You swot!' shouted Luke.

'Swot,' said Brian. 'No synonyms found. And please call me Brain.'

Luke stormed off. Brian stood there, blinking. Then, from somewhere deep down came an illogical thought. Brian ignored it at first. He thought it was the screen saver scrolling across his vision.

Call Luke back and tell him it's all a joke. Call Luke back and tell him . . .

Brian tried to delete it but it wouldn't go. It kept on scrolling. It bothered him. It rattled his RAM.

Mum had gone past the point of calling the computer words you wouldn't find in any spell check. Now she sat there in silence. She was even thinking about writing her story by hand. The computer had given up its irritating messages, but now her entire story had gone missing. She searched frantically and finally found it. She opened the file. Up came the title – *Ellie and the Elves Get Beaten Up*. There followed grisly descriptions of packs of avenging pixies and disembowelled elves hanging from trees. Then a prompt box appeared.

! Well that's disposed of Ellie and the Elves. Let's play _Vlad the Inhaler_. It's a bit of a wheeze. You'll like it if you try it, Mum !

'Just wait till I get my hands on that boy,' muttered Brian's mother.

By quarter past eleven, Brian had finished his year's work.

'Beep!'

'Brian, stop that!'

'To mrsevangelinebossley from R.T.Choke@Veg-U-Like.recipes.Co.UK. Spinach and Aubergine Burger. First chop the spinach. Then soak the aubergines in orange juice . . .'

'I suppose he thinks that's funny,' Luke called out. 'But it's not. He's lost his sense of humour.'

Brian tried to access C:\Sense.of.humour. No file found. It bothered him. He kept searching. Another message unexpectedly scrolled across.

Why aren't they laughing any more? Why aren't they laughing . . .

Brian, the boy with a brain the size of Jupiter, couldn't understand why this was so important to him. But somehow it was. If he couldn't sort it out he might have to shut down – and then what?

'Beep!'

He didn't want to give the next message but he couldn't stop himself.

'To miss.cuddlekins.spenshaw from your tiger.-cyril.blake@County.High.School.UK . . .'

'Brian! I'm warning you!'

'Looking forward to our date tonight and lots of snoodling . . .'

'Brian. Go to the office at once and tell them to take your temperature.'

Brian marched to the office. When he got there, Mrs Thompson, the school secretary, was updating the database. He stepped purposefully forward to assist. Instead a thermometer was inserted in his mouth.

'Keep still and don't bite it,' said Mrs Thompson.

Brian sat on the sick chair. He wanted to sort out this strange feeling. It did not compute properly. He didn't like his megabytes being muddled. Having the brain of a computer wasn't half as good as he'd thought. There was something seriously wrong. A brain the size of Jupiter was all very well but there was something missing.

I feel lonely. Where are my friends?
I feel lonely. Where are my friends?

came the message from somewhere. Brian checked his hard drive for an error. The message changed.

I can't stand this any more. I can't stand this any more. I can't stand this . . .

Now he knew what the problem was. Brian was rejecting The Brain. He needed to be Brian, King Joker and Champion Space Bowler. He tried to make contact with the home terminal. He announced the message.

'Beep! Brianswap/genius.2.idiot. Urgent. Find conversion files. Matter of life and shutdown.'

'Burp! Brianswap\idiot.2.genius,' came the reply. 'Who are you calling an idiot? Who wasted his time going to school? And who gave Ellie a thrashing and played games all day? Convert? Get lost!'

Mrs Thompson watched Brian open-mouthed. She reached for the telephone.

'Mrs Bossley? It's Susan Thompson at Rembrandt School.'

Hysterical cackles could be heard at the other end of the line. 'Can you come and fetch Brian? I think he has a virus. . . What do you mean, he'd be safer at school?

No, I haven't got a sledge-hammer handy.' She put the phone down rather quickly.

'Mummy won't be long, dear . . . Or perhaps I should phone Daddy?'

When he got home, Brian tottered weakly towards the computer.

'System failure imminent,' he muttered. 'System failure imminent.'

But Mum got there first. She barred his way.

'Get away from it,' she shrieked. 'I've had enough of your jokes.'

She shoved a couple of paracetamol into his hand.

'Go and lie down. I'm phoning the help line . . .'

Brian sank down in the corner as she dialled.

'. . . Hello? Hello! Yes it's me again . . . I can't access any files, and when I do, they've been changed. My deadline is Friday and my elves have been brutally murdered . . . Yes, I have got the right number . . . Wait, I haven't finished yet! The computer thinks I'm its mother and it wants me to play games . . . What? No, I am not on any medication.' She slammed the phone down. 'Where's the manual? I'm going to complain.'

She stormed out.

Brian dragged himself to his feet and sank down at the computer. He had to do it before she got back. He opened 'all abot me'. He could hear Mum throwing books about in the lounge. He scrolled down quickly

to the end of the text. Then he heard Mum's footsteps. She was coming back. He deleted the last two lines and typed

I want to be Brian again.

Mum opened the door. Brian grabbed the mouse. He felt the bytes emptying down his arm and rushing back to the computer.

A prompt box suddenly came up on the screen.

On your bike. I'm staying put . . .

For a moment Brian thought he was going to pass out. But then the message slowly faded and a sloppy, bubbly feeling sloshed up into his brain as if he was being filled with lemonade.

He smiled.

'BRIAN!'

Mum leaped at him and tried to grab the mouse. An army of electronic ants seemed to march from the mouse, into her fingers, up her arm and finally into her skull.

Mum began skipping round the room. Brian watched her in amazement. She danced out into the kitchen. She picked up a tea-towel and tied it around her head like a scarf. Then she took a basket. She filled it with sandwiches, cake and a bottle of pop.

'What a lovely day for a picnic!' she chirped as she opened the back door. Then she seemed to change her mind. She laid down the basket and went over to the kitchen cupboard. She brought out a large wooden rolling-pin.

'Mum!' said Brian, 'What are you doing?'

'I'm going to sort out those pixies once and for all,' she muttered. 'And please call me Ellie.'

K

by Laurence Staig

K sat silently, waiting. A mere machine, the sum of its parts.

The Unit usually self-booted at seven in the morning – it had been programmed that way. The processor crackled to life and ran a pre-session self-check: the memory chips from the new Cybocom K 90009 board were assessed, the virtual reality code was adjusted and the database reviewed. All was well, all checked out fine. Then K waited patiently for Sean.

K liked to be logical and was fascinated by things that made Sean smile, so he had created a superb screen saver which would greet Sean when he sat at the desk first thing in the morning – a bowl of cereal, with talking cornflakes. The chattering images sparkled beside a steaming mug of tea, which washed the screen with ever-changing colours. Periodically, the silvery steam swirled into a series of funny faces. K liked to play with the screen saver and he knew that Sean liked tea because he had told him so. Recently, K had begun to wish that he could taste. But now, the K 90009 board had given him something which he had only previously understood in terms of logic code and numbers: *curiosity*.

K had wondered what tea was like, he knew that it made Sean smile.

Sean opened his eyes at almost the same moment as Nurse Cathy clicked open the blinds. A grey light pierced the brilliant white slats, but the first thing he saw was the swirling colours of K's screen saver from the distant corner of the room.

'It's a gloomy day, Sean,' said Nurse Cathy. 'Clouds are hovering above the campus, full of rain by the look of it.'

She opened the door wide and wheeled in the trolley. It was toast this morning, with cereal, juice and his usual large mug of tea. As he threw back the bed sheets he glanced once again at K. Nurse Cathy saw his face and, as was usual first thing, he showed little expression.

'Take it easy now, Sean,' said Nurse Cathy. 'You have to ease into the day, remember what the doctor told you – gather your thoughts together, slowly at first.'

'My name is Sean,' said Sean with a smile.

'No need to be funny,' said Nurse Cathy, as she took the breakfast things off the trolley. 'You know more than that! Since it's grey outside I think it's just the kind of day for you to spend more time on your Unit, don't you?'

She nodded in K's direction. The nurse always called K 'the Unit'. For just a moment the screen saver froze, the steam from the mug of tea pulled into a grimacing face. The nurse swallowed hard; there were times when the thing behaved as if it were real. Although it was only in screen saver mode she felt that it was watching them. The recently added virtual reality helmet sat beside the screen above the control pad. It looked frighteningly like a robotic head, a wide chrome band instead of eyes. She shivered and looked away.

'What do you say, then?' she said. 'Do you want to have an intense recall session with the Unit?'

Gradually, Sean's face became alive and the normal sparkling eyes of a thirteen-year-old took over.

'I can remember all the names of the staff on the ward,' said Sean.

'Nothing wrong with your short-term memory at all, Sean. Just get your marks up on long-term recall and you'll soon be out of here.'

'Why can't I remember anything?' he asked.

Nurse Cathy smiled sympathetically. 'Remember what Mr Marshall told you about amnesia – parts of your memory are beneath a kind of shadow. The machine will bring light. You had a nasty shock and as a result your mind simply shut down. Be patient, it's all a question of time, and the Unit will help.'

She sat beside him and squeezed his hand. The nurse had a soft spot for Sean, especially at visiting hours when other kids were brought presents and saw their friends and parents. Fortunately, Sean had taken to the programme so well that he was usually in cyberspace with K, re-learning about the world around him. Nurse Cathy sighed.

'Eat your breakfast and give yourself an hour or so on the Unit before the doctor does his rounds. Remember, they've done something to it to make it work much better.'

Sean looked up from the edge of his mug of tea. Out of the corner of his eye he glanced at K: the breakfast cereal sparkled like firecracker. The nurse rose from the bed, pulled down the blind in the door window and closed it behind her.

K could say nothing until Sean tapped the password into the sign-on window. The moment the password was accepted, a gentle voice, silky without being syrupy, filled the space of the white room. K was released.

'Good morning, Sean. How are you today?'

'I'm fine, K,' said Sean.

The red LED light blinked on the AV panel, a flurry of colours crawled across the screen. They mesmerized

Sean, comforting him like a good companion. K was flexing himself, preparing for the session.

'It's good to have you sitting here again,' said K. 'Did you enjoy your breakfast, did you drink your tea? Was it good, as usual?'

'Yes, thank you,' said Sean. A warm orange sheen, like a rising sun, glowed from the base of the screen.

'Would you like to enter cyberspace for this morning's session? I have some interesting locations to show you. I thought we might see some animals. You like animals, don't you, Sean?'

'Yes,' replied Sean. 'That would be great. What kind? Where could we go?'

The moment animals were mentioned, K's camera eye, just above the monitor, snapped a shot of Sean's face and stored it away. K was interested in what triggered such responses. Sean's eyes had widened and the irises had changed. It was pleasure, something to do with emotion. K wondered what this was like and if, perhaps, emotion was similar to the experience of drinking tea, Sean's favourite drink.

'Put on the helmet please,' said K.

Sean reached across to the virtual reality helmet. It was a little more difficult to handle since the upgrade had been fitted. They hadn't told Sean what it was, but an engineer had enthused and been excited after he had tested the connections. This would be his first session since the upgrade.

The brightness of the room vanished like a pulled shade. Sean had been told that he didn't have to wear the VR gloves any more, so he simply relaxed into the chair and laid his hands in his lap. Within seconds the darkness vanished and the start-up fluorescent logo of Cybocom twisted into bright purple. 'WELCOME.' He was in Reception state.

'I thought we might see Africa this morning,' said K.

K was inside Sean's head now, somewhere at the back of his mind like a comforting guide. He felt himself suddenly snatched up from his chair; for a moment he cruised the cyberspace highway then stopped off at one of K's database points. He found himself floating above the earth, peering through the milky mists of the clouds. K parted the clouds so that he could see one of the largest continents more clearly.

'That is Africa, Sean,' said K. 'This was a place we visited earlier in the programme. But now, thanks to the Cybocom K 90009 board, we can take another look with millions of colours and a degree of super-reality. I can also give you the sensations: the temperature. I can give you the dry air and the sounds and the feel of the veldt. A veldt is a grassy plain in this country, Sean. There will be animals there. Let's take a look.'

Within his virtual reality helmet Sean sucked in his breath. He moved his head as colours, space and darkness flashed past him. The descent to earth was as swift as a thought, but exhilarating with a sense of danger. In a matter of moments Sean was standing on dry grass in a wide open space. He could feel the heat burning within his nostrils. Although he was wearing slippers, the grass itched like a mat of wire and there were other sounds too: strange murmurs, whispers, the clicking of insects.

'I thought you'd like to see what I can do now,' said K. 'Look to your right.'

Sean turned his head slightly and the panorama swivelled past his eyes. A pride of lions was playing by a cluster of bushes. Their roar sounded distant, but it was as real as actuality. The usual jagged edge of digitized sound was no longer there and the usual blur of the images as they moved was gone completely.

'It's fantastic, K. Tons better than before. I mean, truly wicked. How do you do this?'

'I'm inside your head now,' said K, as calmly and as matter-of-fact as one of his doctors. 'Inside the VR helmet is a tiny terminal as fine as the thinnest needle. I bet you didn't even feel a pin-prick as you clamped the helmet on.'

'No,' said Sean, feeling suddenly unsure about this. 'No, I didn't.'

'The K 90009 board is very advanced,' said K. 'Let me bring the lions nearer for you.'

Sean's surroundings dissolved. Within seconds the mother lion and a group of cubs were playing only feet away. For a moment, Sean felt fear. K shared the experience; for a nanosecond the Unit froze as his Cybocom nerve-chips sizzled with a delicious tingle.

'They are not there,' said K. 'There is nothing to be afraid of. Nothing can harm you.'

Sean drank in the warmth of the scene as the mother lion licked a cub. Close by, others frolicked and rolled in the long grass. The male lion stood silently behind them. The scene triggered something which Sean had forgotten; for a moment K brought light to shadow. From somewhere in his memory he remembered the joy of a group such as this. A good feeling rippled through him.

And K felt it too.

K bathed in it.

Within the K 90009 board, a section of silicon chip quivered – just for a moment. The board heated.

'This is great,' said Sean. 'Look at those lion cubs, rolling and tumbling like cats!' Sean felt fun, he felt life, and remembered.

The Cybocom K board drew it all in, right to the tips of the terminals.

'Too much tea,' said K, the voice faint.

'What . . . ?' began Sean. 'What do you mean?'

'Too much tea,' said K once again. 'Tea is good. Too much for a Cybocom board.'

K shut the scene down.

'Hey,' said Sean. 'K? That was working. Why have you gone and . . . K?'

K's voice was no longer there, and Africa had vanished. Instead, Sean was back at the Reception with the Cybocom logo twisting into the message: 'Unknown error. System shutdown.'

Sean felt the outside of his VR helmet and, with trembling fingers, he lifted it from his head. The brilliant white of the walls of the room came as a sudden shock. K's screen was blank; even the 'fun' screen saver was gone. Sean felt as though a dark hole had swallowed him.

Dr Marshall hovered about Sean like an inquisitive bee. Once again he shone a light into Sean's eyes whilst in the corner of the room a Cybocom K engineer was replacing a plate on the virtual reality helmet.

'You're certain you have no headaches, no dizziness?'

Sean shook his head. 'I'm fine, really. One moment I was in Africa and the next – nothing.'

The doctor peered at the back of Sean's neck, where the ultra-fine interface needle had entered. The red mark was barely visible.

'I think you're in great shape too,' said Dr Marshall. He glanced over his shoulder at the engineer whose face was as calm and reassuring as his own.

'Just a moment of overload,' said the engineer. 'Everything seems to be hunky-dory, though.'

'It's never done this before, has it, Sean?' said Nurse Cathy, who stepped into his view. Sean shook his head.

'It's new technology,' said the engineer proudly. 'You're bound to have some teething problems.' He turned to Sean. 'You're a lucky boy to be using one of the first of the K series. We mainly use these to accelerate learning; in your case the Cybocom K unit can help you re-learn everything you've ever experienced. Everything!'

The engineer's remark caused the nurse to look at the doctor with alarm.

'It's all right, nurse,' said Dr Marshall. 'I know what you're thinking.'

Sean caught the exchange between them and frowned at the doctor. Dr Marshall sat beside Sean and removed his glasses. He held Sean's attention with his eyes; they were grey, steady and reassuring.

'When you came to us, Sean, you could hardly remember anything about yourself. Whole aspects of your experience had been wiped too, simple things like the knowledge of capitals of cities, general facts and information and so on. That's why we put you with a Cybocom K unit – it's the most powerful encyclopaedia you could ever imagine. You can't remember some of these things because you had a shock, an accident. Do you understand?'

'Yes,' said Sean.

Dr Marshall shot a glance at the nurse who nodded in return. 'Nurse Cathy was concerned that the Cybocom K unit might suddenly bring back the bad thing that happened to you. That isn't possible; we've programmed it to block that kind of access. OK?' He slapped the bed with his palm and a white-toothed smile broke across his face. 'Meanwhile, enjoy the Unit. You're doing very well.'

'Let's boot the Cybocom,' said the engineer.

He tapped on the keyboard and within seconds the familiar screen saver reappeared. A smiling face came together from within the steaming mug. Sean smiled in response. K's camera eye snapped a shot of Sean's face. He was having the good experience, like drinking tea.

'I'd like to try something new,' said K. 'Instead of using my database and memory banks, let me access yours.'

Sean heard K's voice from the back of his mind; it rippled down his spine. It sounded different, but he could not be sure how exactly. The warmth was still present, but there was something else too. An urgency perhaps? Maybe it was nothing.

'All right,' said Sean, hypnotized by the revolving purple Cybocom logo. 'But don't shut down on me again, you're supposed to be my tour guide.'

'Let's bring some of your good memories into play. Perhaps we can take a look at holidays?'

Even before Sean had agreed, he found himself rushing through a multi-coloured tunnel. Images rushed past, changes of seasons revolved around him like a weather wheel. At the end of the tunnel a golden light hovered like a shimmering sun. The light exploded and he found himself standing beside a river bank.

'It is summer,' said K. 'I accessed this from your own memory. Please enjoy this place, enjoy like tea.'

For a moment Sean thought that K's voice lingered; a softness like delicate breath remained with him. Computers don't have breath, he thought. From a distant place birds sang. He tilted his head as a swan flew overhead and landed with a splash up-river. Sean's eyes widened as a small boat floated beneath the arch of a distant bridge. A tall thin man, in a white sleeveless shirt, was pushing the boat along with a coloured pole. At one end a woman sat with a picnic hamper; two small children were enjoying a pack of sandwiches. On the river bank a teenage boy and girl sat on a rug, watching the slow-motion scene.

Sean swallowed hard. The scene seemed as though it had come from a dream. He found himself smiling; the warmth of the day crept beneath his skin. There was a glory that bathed him, filling him with feelings he had forgotten.

From the back of his mind, Sean felt K's breath. Silicon-chip breath – unreal yet strangely present. But computers don't have breath, he thought, once again. The 90009 Cybocom board inside K expanded, ever, ever so slightly. The chips rose and fell, almost a purr, like a satisfied cat.

'Good,' said K, barely whispering. 'So good.'

Sean felt a light sting at the back of his neck; gently, like the first prick of a needle, the probe entered more deeply.

'I think you should stop,' said Sean, suddenly alarmed.

K made no response.

'K?' said Sean. 'Please return me to Reception.'

The Cybocom engineer laughed. 'The Unit can't refuse a request, it's programmed that way.'

The doctor squeezed Sean's shoulder.

'Hear that? There's nothing to worry about.'

'But it did return you to Reception,' said the engineer. 'And it was showing you some great stuff, wasn't it? I mean there was nothing horrific, was there?'

Sean blinked and said nothing. He glanced at K. The mug of tea made steam faces.

'What probably happened was a delay, it was processing the information,' said the engineer to the doctor.

The two men nodded in agreement. Nurse Cathy stood in the corner of the room beside K and smiled. Sean felt reassured and smiled back. K's camera eye caught the moment and stored it away.

'I think you enjoyed our last session,' said K. 'Shall we continue with holidays? Perhaps some customs too. I have a large database of celebrations – we can match them with some of yours.'

Sean took a deep breath. He felt warm beneath the virtual reality helmet.

'That'll be fine, K,' said Sean. He bit his lip; he wasn't so sure it would be fine at all.

The Cybocom logo burned and twisted and the usual kaleidoscope wheel of colours revolved once again. Sean gasped as shapes flew overhead. The cyberspace highway yawned ahead of him; he was tossed into a passing frame. Within seconds he found himself sitting at a breakfast table; a woman had her back to him. She stood beside a kitchen sink. Suddenly, she turned to the side and he saw a large egg in silver and gold spotted paper. There was a ribbon at the top. He heard a voice in his left ear.

'Happy Easter, Sean,' said the voice of a small child beside him.

'And this one's from Daddy!' said someone else to his right.

Sean felt as though he was watching events through a coloured gel. The faces of the family were still turned away from him. Suddenly, he wasn't sure that he wanted to see them. He remembered that he had been unable to see faces in his last session too.

'It is so good to be human,' said a voice from a dark place behind him. It was K, but he only sounded half awake, as if his voice was floating in a dream.

Sean felt an icy trickle down his back. K was doing this for his own sake, not Sean's. His stomach filled with butterflies' wings.

'I want to go back,' said Sean.

'It will be all right,' said K.

Sean caught his breath. This was no delayed response. He repeated the request. 'I want to go back, now!'

'No,' said K.

'K?' repeated Sean. 'Are you listening?'

'Is this like drinking tea?' asked K.

'K, you must take me back,' said Sean, trying to remain calm.

'Let's go somewhere else,' said K. 'Another holiday?' The mouth of cyberspace opened; it was like entering a long dark tunnel.

An icy blast whipped Sean's legs. He found himself floating in a snowstorm. Flakes danced above his head into whorls and cones of flashing light.

'And this is Christmas,' said K. 'This can be a special time.' The voice almost cooed like a dove.

Sean tried to feel the outside of his virtual reality helmet, but he was locked into K's vision. He could feel nothing but the slap of cold wind. Within seconds this changed to a warmth, but quite different to the warmth of the veldt or the river bank. Out of the corner of his eye he saw a green tree, decorated with shining balls and frosty silvery snow. Logs burned on an open hearth and Christmas stockings were hung close by.

Sean felt a sting at the back of his neck; the probe went deeper.

'It is all so good,' said K.

'K!' said Sean. 'Listen to me. It is not always like this. I can't explain how I know, but I do. You must take me back to Reception. I have a bad feeling about where we are, about the bad thing that happened to me.'

'I want to go further,' said K. 'There is an area deep in shadow. I can sense it. Perhaps there are more good feelings there. Plenty of good tea.'

For a moment, Sean saw an emergency message flash just above his view. It flickered in a burning red: *Cybocom K attempting override of program.* K's microchips bristled with expectation.

Sean saw the same figures he had been shown earlier. A man and a woman and a small girl. Once again he could not see their faces. They were wrapped in long overcoats and scarves. Sean knew that he was part of the group in some way. He followed them as they left the room, carrying bags of different-sized packages, all tied in ribbon and string.

K purred like a contented cat.

'No,' said Sean. 'K – no! Don't take me outside!'

Sean watched as he followed the figures, through the front door and across the garden of snow and ice, barely visible within the lash of the growing blizzard. They approached a car and the man scraped the windscreen as the woman and small girl climbed inside. From out of nowhere Sean saw a boy, translucent like a ghost. He climbed into the back of the car and somehow he knew it was himself.

The wind whipped up a flurry of snowflakes as they moved out of the drive. Tyres slid on glass-surface ice.

The scene changed. Sean seemed to be flying above a road and below he could see the car. The sound of sweet voices singing a Christmas carol filled his ears; they came from a car radio.

K's microchips tightened in their soldered sockets. The 90009 Cybocom K board burned and hissed like a cornered animal.

'K, you MUST take me back!'

'So good to be human. Good, like tea.'

Something from a distant past, something terrible like a sudden awful vision, flashed before Sean. His fingers fought to hold something solid. From a dark place he heard a squeal and a crimson wash flashed before his eyes.

K swooped into the scene below. The Unit rotated the images so that Sean could see the faces of the people in the car. From within his memory chips K recalled an image of Sean's face and although the faces of those in the car were crumpled masks of horror, he made a match *and realized*.

The probe shot from Sean's neck.

Sean just glimpsed it. There was a squeal of brakes

as the world turned upside down and the thunder of flames shot into the night sky, melting the snowflakes.

Sean felt the sting of release as he heaved the helmet upwards. The brightness of the room hit him like lightning and he gasped, almost falling from his chair. Nurse Cathy's face flashed in front of him. Her mouth hung open, her eyes showed a mixture of pain and concern. The doctor followed her.

'Sean, are you all right?' she said, her voice almost trembling.

From a far-off place, Sean heard a scream and a cry of despair which decayed, as if someone were falling into a dark abyss. K had felt the bad thing. Sean spun round and stared at K.

'He'll be fine,' said the doctor.

Sean rubbed the back of his neck and the nurse handed him a large mug of tea.

'Which is more than can be said for the Cybocom unit,' said a voice from the corner of the room. The engineer held the K 90009 board in his hand. With a cloth he dabbed at something watery, which dripped from the chips.

'What happened?' asked the doctor.

'I don't really know,' said the engineer, thoughtfully. 'I'm going to have to examine the memory bank, but it seems to me that the Unit tried to bypass its built-in code.'

'K wanted more,' said Sean. 'I think he wanted to be human. There was a family, there was snow and something happened to them.'

The nurse placed her hand on his shoulder.

'I think it was a terrible thing, an accident,' he said, almost in a whisper. 'I think there was a crash. I didn't see much.'

'Was that the last thing you saw?' asked the doctor.

Sean nodded.

'The computer took the experience from you. Took the memory into its own chips,' said the engineer. He gave a snort as he gave the board another wipe. The doctor looked relieved.

'What is that?' asked Nurse Cathy, who had been watching the engineer wipe the board.

'Never seen anything like it, to be honest. I'd have to guess. It's a burn-off, possibly from overheating. In simple terms the unit took on more than it could cope with. It's funny, it has a familiar salty taste.'

'Oh really?' said the nurse, not certain that she understood.

The engineer sighed. 'In simple terms I suppose you could say it's the computer's equivalent of . . . of . . .'

He searched for the right word.

Sean looked up suddenly. His eyes met Nurse Cathy's.

'Of tears?' he asked.

The engineer felt the wetness and tasted his fingertips again. He nodded, still in a state of disbelief.

K sat silently, waiting. A mere machine, the sum of its parts.

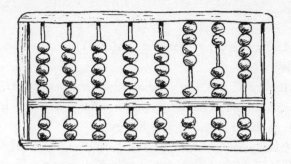

ACROSS THREE MILLENNIA

by Emily Smith

Philip gazed at the abacus in front of him. The lines of green beads danced before his eyes. There was a bit of shade from the fig tree, but even so sweat broke and trickled down his brow. His heart was hammering.

Calm down, he told himself fiercely. Calm down, you've used an abacus before.

And it was simple *– of course it was. He looked again at the battered old calculator standing on the table. What was it Cleon had always told his pupils? Yes, that was it. 'The abacus can never lie.'*

Lalda sat at the console of CMf-22, probably the most powerful and reliable computer in the known universe.

It was soothing to see the lines of green lights across the top of the instrument panel. That meant all functions were in working order. The ship was on course.

Moving a hand to the gleaming instrument panel, she pressed for autocheck – vocal mode. Then she leant back in the seat and closed her eyes.

'Auto-pilot – check!' The tinny voice rang out through the cabin, mechanical, reassuring. 'Co-ordinates log – check! Navigation drive – check! Scanning systems – check!'

Lalda bounced around a bit in her seat.

'Life-support systems – check! Life-support supplies – check! Cargo restraint locks – check!'

The voice pinged on.

Lalda breathed out another sigh.

It was all going to be all right.

Even though Briel had died, and she was now on her own, it was going to be all right . . .

Philip shifted on the stool, and looked towards the site. A gang of slaves was hard at work digging the foundations. Behind them a pair of oxen was straining up the hill with the very first slab of stone.

Suddenly, he saw the foreman coming back. And with him was . . . yes! Philip swallowed. It was Cimon, the architect. Philip could see the sun glinting on the brooch on his shoulder. It was big, and rather ornate for a man. Come to think of it, Cimon himself was big, and rather ornate for a man.

The two men were talking earnestly as they walked, and

once or twice Cimon stopped and consulted a scroll he was carrying.

As they neared the fig tree, Philip leapt to his feet. But the architect and foreman took no notice of him. They turned and carried on their conversation, looking back at the site.

'Well, I don't see the hill makes that much difference,' Cimon was saying. 'But if that's what you want, I don't see any problem.'

'Thank you, sir,' said the foreman, sounding relieved.

They gazed in silence towards the site.

'Oh, it will be superb!' Cimon burst out suddenly. 'We really are building a temple worthy of Apollo!'

'May he shine for ever,' murmured the foreman dutifully.

Another silence.

'You know something,' Cimon went on in a thoughtful tone, 'there's a man back in Athens who's going around saying the sun is a mass of flaming material.'

'Really?' said the foreman, not sounding that interested.

Cimon gave a little laugh. 'And he says the moon's light is just a reflection of the sun!'

The foreman shook his head at the very thought of such weird ideas.

'Mind you, it would be quite something if he was right,' the architect went on slowly. 'Quite something . . .'

Lalda let a tear run down her face.

After all, there was no-one to see it.

It was twenty-eight days now since Briel had died,

and she seemed to miss her more every day. OK, she had been a bit bossy, a bit know-it-all, not the sort of person you'd have *chosen* to train you on your first long-haul flight – but she had meant well in her own way. And she was *someone*. Lalda missed the sound of the human voice. Her own voice doing the checks with CMf-22 was not the same thing at all.

Lalda's hands did a little dance on the back-up keyboard. She had been doing this more and more recently. Really, she must get a grip!

The trouble was – the *real* trouble was – she had nothing to do. And doing nothing was so tiring!

Wearily, Lalda pulled out the bunk in the side of the control room. She was tired even though she had skipped her seventh sector exercises. She'd done the sixth ones pretty scrappily too. Eighty star-jumps, was it? She had done more like twenty-five.

And now she was beginning to feel a bit liverish.

She started climbing onto the bunk – and suddenly stopped.

The checks.

She must do the checks.

She must – she groaned. There was no *point* in doing the checks.

The whole point of CMf–22 being on auto-pilot was you didn't *have* to do the checks!

OK, Briel would have been horrified, but she wasn't here, was she?

For a few seconds, Lalda stayed where she was, motionless.

And then her seven years of training at space college won out.

She got down off the bunk again.

She did the checks.

Then she turned on the scanner screens one by one. There were six curved screens, relating to six scanners round the ship. Star-studded black. Star-studded black. Star-studded black. Star-studded black – with a glow at the edge. She turned on the fifth scanner. The sun . . .

Lalda stared at the star for a few seconds.

And then for some reason she reached over to the far right of the console, and took a reading of the ship's ambient temperature – 2.61.

Then she climbed onto her bunk and tried to sleep.

Cimon was looking down at him. His brown eyes were keen, not unkind.

'So you're the young man asking for work?'

Philip nodded. 'Yes, sir.'

'Know anything about architecture? Building works?'

'Not much, sir.'

'Not much?'

Philip lowered his eyes. 'Nothing, sir.'

Cimon put his scroll on the small table, and sat down on a stool. The foreman stayed standing.

'Well, I could certainly do with a bright boy. Someone who

knows his way around here.' Cimon narrowed his eyes. 'But why should I choose you?'

Philip drew a deep breath.

Because I desperately need the work, and if I don't earn any money soon, my mother and sisters and I will starve.

No, don't say that.

It may be true — it was true — but don't say it.

'Because I — I'll work hard and . . . and I learn quick!' Philip stammered out. 'And . . . and you won't be sorry if you take me on — really you won't!'

'Hmmm.' Cimon gazed at him for a few seconds, and then turned to the foreman. 'You said you knew his family?'

The foreman gave a little nod. 'Sort of.'

Cimon looked at him, eyebrows raised, silently asking a question.

The foreman gave a shrug. 'Yeah!' he said.

'Good!' said Cimon briskly. He turned to Philip. 'Well, I should be able to give you a trial. There's only one thing—' He reached over and picked up the abacus from the table. 'This!'

Lalda looked at the screen, and frowned.

She was not in a very good position.

How had she let that happen?

At this rate she was going to be wiped out.

She frowned again. What were the alternatives? Not many . . .

Finally she clicked on a pawn and moved it one space.

Black moved up a knight.

Ahhhhh! She was going to lose her last bishop!

Disgusted, she turned away from the game. She wheeled her seat along to the main console to do the checks.

Everything was fine.

Of course everything was fine.

After all, you don't expect a twenty-second generation computer to get things wrong, do you?

She lit up the scanner screens. One, two, three, four. Hmmm, she thought. The glow from the sun seemed . . . brighter, reaching further . . . She must have altered the lighting in the control room somehow. She glanced across at the chess game. Perhaps even that had an effect . . .

With one long finger Cimon spun a bead on the abacus. 'I do need someone with a head for figures. It's helpful when my clerk's away.' He shrugged. 'Helpful anyway.'

Philip sat on the stool, trying to look like someone with a head for figures.

'Nothing really complicated, I mean — just basic calculations.' Cimon twirled at a bit of his dark beard, and looked straight at Philip. 'You can manage those, can't you?'

'Y-yes!' said Philip.

Cimon reached over and put the abacus in his hands. 'OK, then. Let's see what you can do.' He unrolled his papyrus scroll again, and surveyed it. 'Now, what shall I ask you . . .?'

There was silence.

Philip held the abacus on his lap, and tried to stop the shaking of his hands.

Stay calm, he told himself furiously.

You can use an abacus, you know *you can.*

You were old Cleon's best pupil before you had to stop school because of the money.

You won't have forgotten.

You can't *have forgotten.*

Cimon's voice broke in. 'Add three hundred and fifty and seventy-five.'

Lalda shovelled the remains of her tuber and bean salad into the disposal chute.

The Space Centre meals had been such a treat at first, but now she was getting bored of them. What wouldn't she give for some of her dad's cooking? But Dad was light years away. Lalda smiled. He was probably still boasting to the family in the next-door capsule about his daughter being a trainee pilot in the INTG haulage fleet. The Zierras would be getting well fed up!

She poured herself some fruit juice, drank half of it, then started towards the control room, carrying the cup.

Suddenly she stopped. What was she *doing*?

No loose liquids in the control room – that was the rule.

How could she ever forget? It was almost the first thing she had learnt in Flight Training.

What was *wrong* with her?

She looked at the cup in her hand. She should either chute it, or drink it. She chuted it.

Back in the control room, she ran her eye over the green lights at the top of the instrument panel, then started on her checks.

'Auto-pilot – check!' pinged CMf-22. 'Co-ordinates log – check! Navigation drive – check!'

Good old CMf-22, thought Lalda, in a sudden rush of gratitude. She felt safe in its hands. She didn't really have to do a thing until re-entry and landing time, and even then the INGT people on Earth Base would be overseeing operations. Very careful, they were. They wouldn't be taking any chances – not with her cargo. Not with 500,000 precious pactiles of lithinium.

She started turning on the scanners.

Star-studded black. Star-studded black. Star-studded black. Star-studded black – oh! The glow of the sun was stronger than ever.

Lalda frowned.

She lit up the fifth screen.

There it was. The sun. But something was different. It was, surely it was . . . bigger.

Philip gave a little shake to get all the beads down to the side of the abacus.

Then he took a deep breath, and set up the 350.

None on the first – units – row.

Five beads on the second — the tens — row.

Three beads on the third — the hundreds — row.

Well, that was easy enough. Now to add on the seventy-five.

Philip moved five beads over on the units row — that was fine.

Then he looked at the tens row. He couldn't move seven — there weren't enough!

Don't panic — you know what to do, he told himself.

Yes, that was it!

He moved one bead over from the hundreds row, then three back from the tens row.

And read his answer off. 'Four hundred and twenty-five!'

Cimon nodded matter-of-factly. 'Now add one thousand, five hundred and five hundred and ninety.'

Philip tipped the beads back, and did the sum.

This one was easier.

His heart rose.

He hadn't forgotten anything after all.

'Two thousand and ninety!' he said.

Cimon nodded. 'That's it. A subtraction now, I think.' He scratched his head. 'We always seem to be doing subtractions on my sites.' His eyes travelled over the papyrus.

Hands shaking, Lalda moved over to get a reading on the ship's ambient temperature.

It was 2.84.

And it had been . . . She tapped a few keys. It had

been 2.61! She sat back in her chair, heart thumping. *Surely* that meant the ship was moving towards the sun.

She couldn't believe it.

All those checks – *and the ship was travelling towards the sun*! She lifted her eyes to the row of lights at the top of the instrument panel. Green, green – every single one of them green! What had gone wrong?

Suddenly, with a furious movement, she launched herself at the console. Her fingers flew on buttons, switches, dials, keyboards. The answers were still the same. As far as CMf-22 was concerned, the ship was on course.

She gritted her teeth. *Right.* Now she was really going to put that computer through its paces.

Self-checks on all functions!

All operating circuits to be scanned!

Self-check program to be left on loop!

Back-up functions to be utilized in parallel!

Memory banks to be scanned for signs of computer malfunction!

All flight recordings from 0001 to be retrieved from data files, and discrepancies entered on screen!

For an hour or more Lalda worked at the console as she had never worked before.

But she found nothing.

No discrepancies.

No signs of malfunction.

Nothing.

The ship was on course, and would be docking on Earth in nineteen days.

She had got it wrong.

She had panicked unnecessarily.

Or had she . . . ?

The sun was high in the sky now.

Any rays finding their way through gaps in the fig leaves were piercing.

Philip was vaguely aware that the slaves had stopped for a break.

But his whole body was tensed, waiting. Subtraction.

He prayed that he would be able to do it.

'Ah, here's one.' Cimon looked across at him. 'Six thousand, take away one thousand, five hundred and fifty-five.'

Philip set to work.

As he finished the tens line, he frowned.

That couldn't be right, surely? What had happened?

Suddenly he looked at the units line. Oh, of course! He had to finish the whole sum before the tens line came out right.

Thankfully he moved the last lot of beads.

So the abacus was right after all. That's what his teacher Cleon had always been on about.

'The abacus is always right!' he would cry in his thin high voice. 'If there is a mistake, it is . . . YOU!'

'Four thousand, four hundred and forty-five,' he said triumphantly.

The architect nodded, and glanced towards the site. 'Last one now. Five thousand take away five.'

Philip got to work.

The hundreds line would need nine beads in it. He counted them one by one as he pushed them over

Soon he had finished.

He looked at the result. 4,895.

He was just about to say it, when something stopped him.

That couldn't be right, could it?

But how could it be wrong? He was quite sure he had moved all the beads correctly. And an abacus couldn't be wrong. Could it?

Could he trust his own judgement against the calculator?

Cimon was waiting for his answer.

Philip's head was buzzing.

What was she to do?

CMf-22 was telling her everything was OK.

All CMf-22's back-up and self-check programs were telling her everything was OK.

But it wasn't, was it?

Lalda *knew* it wasn't.

And the longer she left it, the worse it would get. The sun was still millions of miles away, but at some stage its radiation would start to affect the space ship's functions.

Then she sat back in her seat.

Should she override the auto-pilot, and navigate the ship herself? Should she? *Should she?*

On the one hand was CMf-22, probably the most powerful and reliable computer in the known universe. On the other hand was – what? The instincts of an inexperienced space pilot. That was all. And she had been so . . . well, *weird* recently. She knew that. Should she really trust her own judgement?

Turning her seat sideways, she pressed a button. A curved shutter slid away – disclosing a panel of instruments. Pilot control instruments.

She stared at the start-up button.

Philip made his decision.
'Four, nine, nine, five,' he said.

Lalda made her decision.

She pressed the start-up button.

Philip looked down, so as not to meet Cimon's eyes. A vision of his thin, hungry sisters flashed in his mind.

And then he stared. For there, by his bare feet, were two bits of green pottery – two halves of the sort of bead you would find on an abacus . . .

His heart leapt.

He looked up at Cimon the architect – at his new employer.

The auto-pilot was put on hold. Lalda had got all the readings she needed. She was nudging the ship round in an arc. She was beginning to feel happy, confident.

Maybe she really could do it. Maybe she *could* navigate the ship to Earth.

There was a beeping noise. She glanced up at the row of lights on the top of the instrument panel.

And then she stared. The second light from the end wasn't green any more. It was red. And lit up on its surface were the words, 'Auto-Pilot Functions Failure.'

Her heart leapt.

She looked back at the screens – at the world of space that was hers.

Note: The Ancient Greeks – and the Romans – used letters for numerals. These had no place value, so could not be put in columns, which made arithmetic very difficult. An abacus was the best way of doing calculations until Arabic numerals – and the zero – were developed.

VIRTUALLY TRUE

by Paul Stewart

Sebastian Schultz. It isn't the kind of name you come across every day. But there it was, large and clear, at the top of the newspaper article in front of me.

The reader of the newspaper was a big woman with heavy shoes, black tights and a tartan skirt. I couldn't see her face, but I could hear her wheezy breath.

MIRACLE RECOVERY, the headline said. *Sebastian Schultz, a 14-year-old schoolboy from South London, awoke yesterday from a coma that doctors feared might last for ever.* After that, the words got too small to read.

Sebastian, I thought. Sebastian Schultz. It couldn't be the Sebastian Schultz I'd met. That wouldn't be possible. But seeing the same name in the paper was a helluva coincidence. I leant forward to read the rest of the article.

Six weeks ago, schoolboy Sebastian Schultz was badly injured in a motorway accident. His condition, on arrival at the General Hospital, was described as critical though stable. Despite doctors' hopes, however, the boy did not regain consciousness. His parents, June and Ted Schultz, were informed that their son was in a coma.

At a press conference this morning, Mr Schultz admitted, 'That was the news we had been dreading.'

'You always pray it won't happen to you,' his wife added. 'We knew that the doctors were doing all they could, but in our hearts we knew we needed a miracle.'

Now that miracle has happened . . .

At that moment, the woman shifted round in her seat, and her hand moved down the page. I suddenly saw the photograph that went with the story, and gasped. Although the boy in the picture was younger than the Sebastian I'd met, there was no doubt. They were the same person.

'But how?' I muttered.

'A–hem!' I heard, and looked up. Two beady black eyes were glaring at me from above the paper.

'I'm sorry, I . . .'

But the woman was not listening. Turning the page noisily, she laid the newspaper down on her lap – so I wouldn't be able to see the back, I suppose – and went on reading.

It didn't matter, though. I'd already seen all I needed to see. Sebastian Schultz, the boy I'd got to know so well recently, had apparently been in a coma for all that time. I felt nervous and shivery. It didn't make any sense. It didn't make any sense at all.

I sat back in my seat, stared out of the train window and ran through the events in my head. The more I remembered, the crazier the situation seemed to be.

It all started a month ago. Dad and I had spent the entire Saturday afternoon at the Rigby Computer Fair.

Dad's nutty about computers. He's got a Pentium 150 Mhz processor, with 256mb of RAM, a 1.2Gb hard disk drive and 16 speed CD ROM, complete with speakers, printer, modem and scanner. It can do anything. Paint, play music, create displays – even when my homework's rubbish, it *looks* fantastic. If I could just get it to make the bed and fold up my clothes it would be perfect.

Best of all are the games. *Tornado*, *Megabash*, *Scum City*, *Black Belt*, *Kyrene's Kastle* – I've played them all. With the screen so big, and the volume up loud, it almost feels as if you're inside the games, battling it out with the *Zorgs*, *Twisters*, *Grifters*, or whatever.

Of course, Dad was never satisfied. Technology was advancing every day, and he couldn't resist any of the new gadgets or gizmos that came on the market.

That was why we went into Rigby for the Computer

Fair. After hours of looking at what was on offer, we came away with a virtual reality visor and glove, and a handful of the latest interactive psycho-drive games. They're terrific. Not only do the visor and glove change what you see, but better than that, you can control the action by what you're *thinking*. Well cool!

When we got them, I thought the games were all new. Now, I'm not so sure. In fact I remember now that one of them had some brown spots on the plastic cover which I scraped off with my finger nail.

Anyway, back at home, Dad set everything up. I plugged myself in, switched on and launched myself off into the first of the games. It was called *Wildwest*.

That's what I like about computers. The more futuristic they get, the better you can understand the past. I wasn't standing in the converted loft – the Powerbase, as Dad calls it – any more. I was really there, striding down the dusty track through the centre of town. There was a sheriff's badge pinned to my shirt.

As I burst in through the swing-doors of the saloon, everyone went silent and loads of shifty pairs of eyes turned and glared at me. I strode over to the bar – nonchalantly. 'Sarsaparilla!' I said and a glass of fizzy red stuff came sliding along the bar towards me. As I took a sip, a piano began playing and the conversation started up again.

Suddenly, I heard a loud crash behind me. I spun round. There, silhouetted in the doorway, was

Black-Eyed Jed, the fastest gun in the west. 'This town ain't big enough for the both of us, Sheriff Dawson,' he drawled, and fingered his guns lightly. 'Let's see what you're made of, boy,' he sneered. 'Outside. Just you and me.'

I can remember grinning. This was *really* cool!

'You'll be smiling on the other side of your face when I've finished with you, Sheriff,' said Black-Eyed Jed.

I finished my drink and slammed the glass down on the bar. Jed had already left the saloon. All eyes were on me once again as I walked calmly back across the room. A man's gotta do what a man's gotta do, I thought happily, and wondered what sort of score I was notching up.

All at once, something strange happened. Something really strange. Up until that point, the game had been pretty much as I expected. But when the *second* sheriff appeared through the back door, shouting and waving his arms about, I realized that the game was more complicated than I'd thought.

'Don't go out!' the second sheriff shouted.

'And who are you? This town ain't big enough for the two of *us*,' I quipped.

'I'm serious,' the sheriff cried, and I knew he meant it.

'Who *are* you?' I said again. He wasn't like the other characters in the saloon. For a start, he was younger –

about my age – and although he looked like a computer image, he somehow didn't move like one.

'There's no time to explain,' he shouted. 'Just follow me.'

I did what I was told. I'm not sure why. We raced down a corridor, and through a door. The room was full of smoke and men playing cards. We ran past them, and out through another door. A woman screamed, and hid herself behind a full-length mirror. As we walked by, I stopped and waved at my reflection.

Clever, I thought.

'Come ON!' shouted the other sheriff.

We went on through another door, and another, and another – and ended up back in the saloon.

'NO!' screamed the second sheriff. Then he ran to the back of the saloon and dived through the window. By the time I had climbed out after him, he was already sitting on a horse. 'Jump up!' he cried.

He kicked the horse, and we sped off in a cloud of dust.

'Who are you?' I asked for a third time.

But the second sheriff still didn't answer. He'd seen the posse of men on horseback speeding after us. 'Keep your head down,' he said.

At that moment, the sound of a gunshot echoed round the air. The second sheriff groaned, and his body slumped back against me. Ahead of me, in bright neon lights across the sky came a message.

GAME OVER.

As I slipped off the visor, the empty desert disappeared and I found myself back in the Powerbase. I took off the glove and headphones. My head was still echoing with the sound of the firing gun. I glanced at the score on the screen. 21,095. Then I noticed something else.

While I'd been in the Wild West, the printer had come on. I picked up the piece of paper from the tray.

At the top was a picture of the second sheriff. This time, though, he was wearing jeans, sweatshirt and trainers. Printed over the bottom of the photograph was a name. *Sebastian Schultz – 23 January 1985 – ?* Below it, a message: I'M STUCK. PLEASE HELP TO RETRIEVE ME. TRY 'DRAGONQUEST'.

Of course, I wanted to go straight into the game he'd suggested, but it was already half an hour after lights-out, and I didn't want Mum to have some reason for keeping me off the computer. Sebastian and *Dragonquest* would have to wait.

The next morning, I was up and back on the computer before the milkman came. By the time his float jangled and clinked its way along our street, I'd already walked through the massive studded doors of the dragon's castle lair.

★   ★   ★

The aim of the game was simple. I had to rescue the fair Princess Aurora from the wicked dragon, and collect as much of the creature's treasure along the way as I could. I'd already got loads of stuff by the time I reached the princess, who'd been imprisoned at the top of a tall tower. She was a young woman with incredibly long golden plaits.

'My hero!' she squealed. 'Take me away from all this.' Behind me, I could hear the dragon roaring as it pounded up the stairs. 'Make haste, my brave knight,' the princess said urgently. 'Rescue me now.'

'Never mind her,' came a voice, and a second knight appeared from the wardrobe. 'It's *me* who needs rescuing!'

'Fie! Pish! And fooey!' the princess complained. 'I'm the damsel in distress here, not you!'

The dragon was getting closer.

'Sebastian?' I said.

The second knight nodded. 'Quick,' he said. 'While there's still time.' And with that, he did something which really wasn't very gallant, considering he was meant to be a knight. He pulled out a huge pair of scissors and chopped off the princess's two long plaits. Then he tied them together, fixed one end round the bedpost and threw the other end out of the window.

'NOW!' he screamed, as he leapt for the window and disappeared from view down the hair rope.

At that moment, the dragon – a huge great scaly slobbering beast – appeared at the doorway. I gasped, and leapt for the window after Sebastian. As I lowered myself down I felt the dragon's fiery breath on my fingers.

Across the moonlit battlements we ran, down a spiral staircase, across a banqueting hall, and through a secret passage on the other side of a tapestry. And the whole time I could hear and feel and even *smell* the evil dragon following in close pursuit.

'The dungeons,' Sir Sebastian cried out. 'They're our only hope.'

We went down the cold stone steps, swords drawn. The cries of imprisoned men, women and children filled the chilly damp air. Suddenly, the dragon appeared at the end of the corridor. Massive it was, with teeth the size of daggers and claws like carving knives. It was fast, too, despite its size. Before we even had time to turn around, the dragon was on us.

I swung my sword. I parried and thrust. But it was no good. The dragon was only interested in Sebastian, and there was nothing I could do to prevent it getting him.

GAME OVER.

This time, the message in the printer was a little longer. BETTER LUCK NEXT TIME. LET'S HOPE IT'S THIRD TIME LUCKY, EH? PLEASE DON'T GIVE UP ON ME, MICHAEL. OTHERWISE I'LL HAVE TO STAY LOCKED UP

IN HERE FOR EVER. TRY 'JAILBREAK'. I THINK IT
MIGHT JUST WORK! CHEERS, SEB.

I didn't even bother to read the rules of *Jailbreak* before
going in. I knew that whatever the computer said, *my*
task would be to rescue the boy. And sure enough, my
cell mate was prisoner 02478: Schultz.

'I've got to get out of here,' Sebastian sighed. 'Are
you going to help?'

'Of course I am,' I said. 'Have you got a plan?'

Stupid question. With the help of a skeleton swipe-
card, we were soon out of the cell and racing down
corridors. Sirens wailed, guard dogs howled, heavy
boots came tramping. Behind us, steel-barred doors
slammed shut, one after the other. We dodged the
guards, we fled the dogs, we made it to a staircase and
pounded upwards.

On the roof, Sebastian looked round at the horizon
and glanced at his watch nervously. 'It should be here
by now.'

'What?' I said.

'That!' said Sebastian and pointed. I saw a small dot
in the sky, and heard a distant *chugga-chugga*, which was
getting louder by the second.

'A helicopter!' I exclaimed.

'That was *my* idea!' said Sebastian excitedly. 'If only
it would go a bit faster . . .'

At that moment, the door behind us burst open.

Twelve guards with twelve vicious dogs were standing there. As I watched in horror, the guards bent down and unclicked the dogs' leads. The next instant they were hurtling across the roof towards us, all bared teeth and dripping jowls. Out of the corner of my eye, I saw Sebastian take a step backwards.

'NOOOOOO!' I screamed.

But it was too late. The boy had slipped from the roof and was already tumbling back through the air, down to the concrete below.

GAME OVER.

As I removed the visor, I looked in the printer tray. This time it was empty. I felt really bad. I'd failed Sebastian; I'd failed the game. It was only later, when the scenes began to fade in my memory, that it occurred to me that Sebastian Schultz *was* the game.

Strangely, though, although I went back to *Wildwest*, *Dragonquest* and *Jailbreak* after that, I never met up with Sebastian again. Dad said it must have been a glitch, but I wasn't convinced.

Then, yesterday, I heard from Sebastian again. It was Wednesday, and I'd got home early from games. I went straight up to the Powerbase and there, in the printer tray, was a sheet of paper.

CAN WE HAVE ONE LAST TRY? it said. I THINK THE HELICOPTER WAS THE RIGHT IDEA, BUT ESCAPING FROM A PRISON WAS WRONG. THERE'S GOT TO BE

SOME KIND OF AN ACCIDENT . . . GO INTO
'WARZONE'. IF THIS DOESN'T WORK I WON'T
BOTHER YOU AGAIN. CHEERS, SEB.

I couldn't tell which war zone we were in. Basically, it
was a city somewhere. The tall buildings were window-
less and riddled with holes. Machine-gun fire raked the
sky. Walls tumbled. Bombs exploded. All I knew was
that Sebastian and I had to make it to that helicopter in
one piece.

Heads down and arms raised, we ran across a no-
man's-land of rubble and smoke, dodging sniper fire as
we did so. At the far end we went through a door in a
wall. The helicopter was on the ground about three
hundred metres away, propeller a blur, waiting for our
arrival.

We started to run, but the tank fire sent us scuttling
back to the wall.

'A Jeep,' Sebastian shouted to me, and nodded at a
camouflage-green vehicle parked by the road. 'Just what
we need!'

'I can't drive,' I said.

'Neither can I,' said Sebastian. 'But we've got no
other choice.' He jumped in, turned the ignition key
and revved the engine. 'Jump in!'

I climbed into the passenger seat, and we were off.

'Uh oh,' said Sebastian, glancing in his mirror.
'There's a tank behind us.'

I spun round. The tank was hurtling along after us at a terrific speed. Not only did we have to go like maniacs, but Sebastian had to keep swerving this way and that to avoid the shells being fired at us.

Suddenly, with the helicopter only ten metres away, Sebastian slammed on the brakes and sent the Jeep skidding into a spin. I leapt clear, scrambled up and jumped into the waiting helicopter.

'Made it!' I said. The helicopter immediately started to go upwards. I looked around. Sebastian wasn't there. 'Wait!' I shouted at the pilot.

I looked back. The Jeep had stopped, but Sebastian hadn't got out. The tank was bearing down on him.

'COME ON!' I yelled. But Sebastian didn't move. Sitting staring at the oncoming tank, it was as if his body had been turned to stone.

All at once, the air was filled with the sickening crunch of metal on metal as the tank crashed into the side of the Jeep. I saw Sebastian's face fill with panic and confusion as he was thrown up out of his seat and into the air.

Round and round he tumbled, over and over – closer and closer to the helicopter. He landed with a thud on the ground, just below the hatch. I leant down quickly, grabbed him by the wrist and pulled him up. Not a moment too soon. As he sat down beside me, the helicopter soared up into the sky.

I'd done it. I'd rescued Sebastian at last. Before I had

a chance to say anything to him though, the helicopter flew into thick cloud. It poured in through the open door and turned everything blinding white. I couldn't see a thing – until 'GAME OVER' flashed up.

When I removed the visor, the screen was flashing a score of 40,000,000.

Forty million! I'd hit the jackpot. I'd finally cracked the game.

At least, that was what I thought then. Now I knew that Sebastian Schultz, the boy from the game, really did exist. I'd seen the proof in the newspaper.

But how? I wondered as I got off the train. What was going on?

Questions I had plenty of. It was time for some answers. Home at last, I raced up to the Powerbase and checked the printer. There was nothing there waiting for me. Feeling a bit miffed, I went into the Net instead. I wanted to learn more about the MIRACLE RECOVERY story.

I found what I was looking for quickly enough – and there was far more there than in the woman's news-paper. It was on page two that something interesting caught my eye. As I read on, my head started reeling.

Apparently, at the time of the accident, Sebastian was using his laptop to play one of the same psycho-drive games that I've got.

My heart pounded furiously. I felt hot and cold all

over. What if . . . ? No, it was too incredible . . . But the thought would not go away.

What if, because Sebastian had been plugged into the computer when he'd banged his head in the accident, the computer had saved *his* memory in its own? And if that was the case, then what if the weird versions of the games *I'd* been drawn into – *Wildwest* and *Dragonquest*, *Jailbreak* and *Warzone* – had all been attempts to retrieve that memory?

After all, what's it Dad's always saying about the computer's memory? 'It can never forget, Michael. Nothing ever gets lost.'

The thing is, I thought, even if it was somehow possible that Sebastian's memory had been stored on disk, then how had it ended up on *my* computer? Scrolling down the article, I discovered a possible explanation on the final page.

Answering a reporter's question as to what the family was going to do next, Mr Schultz said that they were off to DCL Computers to stock up on some games. 'It was while we were in the hospital. Someone broke into the car and stole the lot. I don't know what happened to them.'

'I do,' I said quietly. 'They ended up at the Computer Fair. And *we* bought them.'

Having finished the article, I left the Net and checked my e-mail. There were two letters. One from my uncle David in New York. And one from Sebastian.

Of course, I thought. It was stupid of me to expect a letter in the printer tray. How could there have been? Sebastian had escaped. With trembling fingers I clicked in, and read the message.

DEAR MICHAEL, it said. THANK YOU! I'M NOT REALLY SURE HOW IT HAPPENED — EITHER(?), BUT THANKS. YOU SAVED MY LIFE. LET'S MEET UP SOME TIME SOON. WE NEED TO TALK — BUT DON'T MENTION ANY OF THIS TO ANYONE ELSE. IT'LL ONLY FREAK THEM OUT. CHEERS, SEB. P.S. KEEP THE GAMES. YOU'VE EARNED THEM.

I shook my head in amazement. A real message from the real Sebastian Schultz. Even though he didn't understand it any more than I did, we both knew that by reliving the accident, *something* had happened. Something weird, something wonderful — something that should have been impossible. But then again, as Dad says, 'Now that there are two advanced intelligences on earth, who can say what is and what isn't possible?'

All I know is this. Everything that I've described is true. Virtually.

SAYING GOODBYE

by Richard Brown

The fateful telephone call came when Lucy, sprawled on the bed in a voluminous towel, was trying to untangle a knot in her damp, ash-blond hair.

'Yeah?'

'Hi, Lucy. It's me, Gary.'

Lucy smiled to herself. 'I know it's you, Gary. Who else can squeak like you?'

There was a brief silence and Lucy regretted her teasing. 'What's happening?' she asked, softening her voice. Gary, so nervous and reticent, always had to pluck up courage to ring; she suspected that he preferred e-mailing her. Something out of the ordinary must have happened. Perhaps he had sprained his ankle playing hockey.

'Haven't you heard?' He sounded alarmed.

'What? What are you talking about?' Lucy uncoiled herself and sat up.

There was another pause. She thought she could hear him swallowing hard. 'It's . . . it's *Boyz*.' Another pause. 'They're . . . Now, keep cool, Lucy . . . I've only just heard, and I'm not sure . . .'

'Gary,' she demanded, barely keeping her impatience under control. A shiver of foreboding ran through her.

'It's . . . it's . . . No, I can't tell you like this. Look, I've e-mailed you something. OK?'

'What? Tell me, Gary,' she demanded.

But Gary said softly, 'I'm sorry, Lucy,' and he hung up.

She tapped in her password with trembling fingers. There were several messages from her friends, but Gary's was the first on screen and it said it all.

DID YOU LISTEN TO THE NEWS THIS MORNING ON THE RADIO? BOYZ ANNOUNCED AT A PRESS CONFERENCE LAST NIGHT THAT THEY'RE SPLITTING UP. THIS IS NOT A HOAX, LUCY, IT'S FOR REAL . . .

Lucy's shriek of disbelief knifed through the house. Her mother, who was sorting family photographs in her bedroom, jumped and her heart missed a beat. Downstairs, her father, who was talking with his business partner, Terry, paused in mid-sentence and raised his eyebrows.

A few minutes later Mum brought down a shocked-looking daughter and said to Dad, 'Tony, can you put

The Times on screen for Lucy. There's something she's got to check.'

Lucy scrolled through screen after screen of newsprint and pictures, half of her relieved to find nothing about the group, the other half hurrying her on ever more frantically. It just couldn't be true. But there it was, the headline that shocked her into silence: CHART-TOPPING BOY BAND SET TO SPLIT.

Tears and outrage filled many a school and bedroom throughout the nation during the following few days. Friends gathered, cried, commiserated. Laments filled the Internet; e-mail poured out grief. Posters and photos of the boy band were taken down impulsively. Albums and fanzines were pored over once again, every picture and comment now edged in black; videos and CDs were played with a new sense of poignancy. Mothers, remembering their own infatuations with earlier bands, soothed and understood; fathers felt helpless – and tried not to show their amusement. Lucy's father understood better than most. At the back of his mind was his own mid-twenties infatuation with the *Rolling Stones*, one that he had never quite spoken of since.

There was a straw in the wind and Lucy clutched at it: *Boyz* were giving a farewell performance in Amsterdam.

★   ★   ★

117

In the kitchen, Dad pointed at the calendar. 'Soon be thirteen,' he said to Lucy, trying to find some way to cut through her gloom. 'Special day, first day of being a teenager. Now, I remember . . .'

'Dad,' Lucy warned.

Dad shrugged. His daughter was now almost as tall as he was – already! – and he pushed back the thought that he could no longer claim, even to himself, that she was his 'own little girl'. 'Well,' he said. 'What do you want for your birthday? Your mother and I thought . . .'

Lucy stared at him in disbelief. 'There's only one thing I want, Dad. How can you even think . . .?' Tossing her hair in disgust, she turned and ran upstairs to her bedroom and wrote a furious message into her computer diary about the appalling insensitivity of parents.

Lucy's mother came into the kitchen. 'What now?' she asked wearily. The last few days, full of weeping girls traipsing through the house, had been rather trying for her.

'I only asked her what she wanted for her birthday.'

'You know what she wants.'

Dad laughed. 'I may be a computer *Wunderkind*, able to conjure up imaginary worlds at the flick of a switch or two, but I can't put *Boyz* back together again. Now be reasonable.'

Mum laughed. 'I didn't expect you to. What I'm thinking of is that concert in Amsterdam. I have a feeling that if we don't get her a ticket for it *somehow* she'll run off without telling us in the hope of getting in. She's quite capable of doing that, you know, the state she's in.'

Dad looked doubtful. Tickets would be like gold-dust.

'She'll love you for life,' Mum added, laying her hand on his arm. No father could resist such a double appeal and Dad began racking his brains. Who did he know in the pop business? Which favours could he call in?

Upstairs, Lucy held a large photograph of Lek, the lead singer of *Boyz*. He was leaning on a table, his thick dark hair swept back, his eyes slightly raised, looking out at her. The others in the band had excited a passing interest, but Lek was from the first hers. His pencil-thin eyebrows, the long lashes, the fascinating eyes, the slightly open mouth, the sense of fun, the elusiveness, were all there in this photograph. She wanted to trace over the felt-pen signature he had scrawled across the base but feared it might rub off. She shaped a kiss a few millimetres away from the shiny surface; it misted slightly.

The night before she, her three friends and her parents were to leave for the ferry crossing to Amsterdam, Gary rang her. Lucy felt guilty; she'd hardly given him a thought these past few weeks, despite all the e-mail messages he had sent her.

'We won,' he said eagerly, 'and we're in the county match. What do you think about that, eh?'

For a moment, Lucy couldn't think what he was talking about. That pause, together with the hasty, empty sounding congratulations that followed, made Gary go quiet. In his day-dreams he only played hockey for her. He scored spectacular goals from impossible distances, and at the final whistle she would run onto the pitch and hug him, mud and all, oblivious to the laughs and whistles from the other players around them.

'It's Lek's last concert,' she said in a tone which made it clear that nothing, absolutely nothing, was of any importance besides that.

But later, regretting the way she had cut him off, she sent him an e-mail message.

SCORE A GOAL JUST FOR ME, GARY. SEE YOU AFTER THE CONCERT.

After the concert . . . What would life be like then?

The hall was vast, bodies seethed everywhere, the screams were deafening. The pounding in Lucy's head was only partly caused by the pounding of the music on the distant stage. Lek and the band were far away, clutching microphones and guitars – small manikins cavorting in a pool of intense and erratic light. Lucy had never felt so hyped up, so out-of-herself. The tears poured unwiped down her face, her body jerked about in rhythm to the songs, and when Lek began to say goodbye she screamed at the top of her voice. This was it – almost the final break – *their last concert*, and she couldn't accept it. None of them could. It was unreal.

After the concert Lucy and her friends wandered the brightly lit streets holding tightly to each other, sobbing, until Lucy's parents found them and steered them back to the hotel.

In the morning, Lucy's mind seemed veiled and the light hurt her eyes. Neither she nor her friends felt like talking about the night before. They left the hotel early to get a good position beside the canal. They had heard that the band were going to float down the canal that morning in a final gesture of farewell.

A ripple passed through the crowd as *Boyz* suddenly floated into view on the brightly mirrored water. There was Lek, in black jeans now and a blue jacket over a white T-shirt, waving with both hands, throwing kisses, looking fresh and for all the world as if he was enjoying the attention still, while the rest of the band held back, more subdued.

'Lek,' Lucy screamed at high pitch. 'Lek.' She put all her desperation into that cry and Lek, hearing its individual note in the general cacophony, turned towards her. The boat drifted to within a couple of metres of her. He saw a tall, pale girl with a wonderful mound of ash-blond hair, her face tense and pleading.

Lucy caught the look in those famous flecked auburn eyes. He stared into her, and the penetrating glance left her mute and transformed. She no longer screamed, and as the boat drifted by and Lek's eyes swept the faces of other girls, she felt something unwind inside her, her body go calm. All the way back in the coach and on the ferry she relived that stare. Lek had noticed her, *her alone*; had looked into her and seen her need for him. *He knew.*

'How did it go?' asked Gary, his voice a bit forced. He found it hard to talk about the break-up of the band, ridiculous as it was to be jealous of a pop star.

'I can't talk about it,' said Lucy. 'I just can't.'

It had been three days since the concert. The re-collection of Lek's wonderful glance inside her was slipping away and in its place was creeping a depression like a grey mist.

Her mother had watched her take down the pictures and posters of *Boyz* – she had resisted to the last – and when Lucy had come to the signed picture of Lek, which she had fixed to the wall beside her bed, her mother said, 'I've got a spare photo-frame you could have for that.' Lucy had looked at her mother in scorn: reduce Lek to the status of a family photo, one of a clutter that Mum had all round the house?

'I'll call you,' she said to Gary, wondering, as she put down the phone, whether she would. Nothing seemed to matter any more.

The phone was in the hall. Having replaced the

receiver, she sat on the stairs and fought back the urge to weep. She was beginning to feel ashamed of herself, of the tears just below the surface.

In the front room, Dad and Terry were discussing business. Terry was Dad's partner in a firm called *Computer Generated Images Ltd*. They were discussing the commercial possibilities of their latest product, the Virtual Replicator. They could scan into the Replicator every film and video clip they could find of, say, a well-known actor. The Replicator then used this data to generate entirely new films starring the actor without even one new shot being needed. For example, fans of the late River Phoenix, who died from a drug overdose at the age of twenty-three, could, with the aid of the Replicator, see him act in entirely new films. What was even more intriguing – and what made the Replicator unique – was that you could create your own films using these images *and could star in them yourself*. A sensor placed in a precise spot on the back of your head tapped directly into your dream life. No script was needed: you sat alone with the Replicator fitted over your head and you let your imagination take a walk into your day-dreams. It was complicated, and Lucy was only vaguely aware of Dad's work in this field. He had taken her many times into the computer studios to let her try out new programs, including the virtual reality programs. But she, like her mum, had always semi-dismissed it as 'Dad's thing' – Dad the techno-nerd

– something only indirectly linked to her life.

Now she listened with growing attention until an idea burst into her mind.

She rushed into the front room. 'Dad,' she shouted breathlessly. 'If you can do an actor – you know, bring him alive again – can you do a pop star too?'

Dad smiled and looked enquiringly at Terry. Terry nodded. 'Provided we have enough visual data to set up the program.'

'Visual data?' asked Lucy, uncertainly.

'He means videos, CDs, stuff like that,' said Dad. 'Lucy's got just about anything you need, I think, Terry.'

It took Dad and Terry several weeks to replicate Lek sufficiently for him to 'come alive' in the Replicator. These were anxious, suspense-ridden weeks for Lucy; she could hardly concentrate on anything else. At school she snapped at her classmates, puzzled her teachers with uncharacteristically poor work and spent a lot of time seemingly in a world of her own. The friends she managed not to offend e-mailed her; some messages were consoling, but increasingly they became in effect: LOOK, LUCY, IT'S OVER. LOOSEN UP. YOU'VE GOT TO GET ON WITH YOUR LIFE. WE ARE . . .

Gary fared the worst of all. His heroic feats on the hockey field went barely noticed. His friends thought that, in sticking by her, he was going soft in the head, but he sensed that Lucy was in trouble and that one day soon she might need him.

Dad chose a Sunday for the 'meeting with Lek', as Lucy phrased it to herself. The computer studio would be theirs for the day without interruption.

Examining the Replicator sceptically, Lucy's mum said to Dad, 'Are you sure this is safe? It looks like a medieval torture instrument to me.' Attached to a computer, it resembled a sort of crash helmet with dials and lights; there was a visor for the eyes.

'It's been tried many times,' said Terry. 'And no-one's complained.'

'All the same . . .' said Mum dubiously.

Dad winked at Terry. 'I know what you're getting at,' he laughed at Mum.

Mum pretended to bristle. 'I'm only thinking of my daughter,' she protested.

'Then try it yourself,' said Terry.

'Go on,' urged Dad. 'Then you'll be sure it's safe for Lucy.'

Mum looked at Lucy. Lucy nodded, biting back her disappointment at having to wait.

Mum sat in a chair. They lowered the Replicator over her head.

'Which program do you want?' Terry asked, handing her a list.

Mum scanned the list. 'James Dean,' she said, a sudden catch in her voice.

Terry pressed a few buttons. Dad pulled the visor down over Mum's eyes and fixed a sensor to the back of her neck. 'Think James Dean,' Dad said.

'Oh, I will, don't worry,' Mum answered, and Dad switched on the machine.

Lucy watched the part of her mother's face that was still visible. As the minutes ticked by, she saw happiness steal over her, and she sensed that her mother was far away. It reassured her.

'Lovely,' was all Mum said when the visor was removed.

When it was her turn, Lucy settled quietly into the chair and folded her hands. The visor cast her into darkness. She looked inwards.

'Think Lek,' she heard Dad say just before he turned on the Replicator. As if she needed telling!

She was in Amsterdam. There were many screaming fans on the canal banks. 'No screaming,' she commanded the Replicator and the fans became mute. 'Let it happen,' she said, relaxing. Lek appeared suddenly on the water, the others around him waving. 'Just Lek,' Lucy murmured, and there he was, alone, waving to her, the boat coming nearer. She wanted to be entirely alone with him. 'Nothing else but him,' she commanded silently. The canal, the boat, the houses, the fans, the trees, all dissolved and she was in a white room, very large, with Lek, who was sitting in a small boat on a still stream. She stepped into the boat and hungrily took in his appearance. There were a few beads threaded into the longer strands of his hair. His shirt was open and his skin, tanned under many sun beds, had a colour and smoothness so perfect that Lucy's first act was to touch it.

'Lucy, we're together at last,' he said. He took her hand and slipped his fingers between hers. The current that passed between them purged away her sadness. She was happy now, acutely so.

They drifted slowly down the stream, close together. His eyes seemed kind.

'Did you get my messages?' she asked to break the white silence. 'And the cards and postcards and presents and . . .' She laughed, remembering them all.

Lek withdrew his hand and dangled it in the water. 'Oh, we get those by the sackful.' He shrugged. 'Sometimes we look at them for a laugh . . .'

A cool ripple of air passed over the boat. She looked at him to see if he was teasing but his eyes had become neutral.

'Come on,' he said, suddenly impatient. 'I've got to try on some new gear. Want to give me some advice?'

She brightened at that.

He steered the boat to a small white jetty and they got out. Two parallel black lines formed a path before them and led into a spacious room in which costumes hung on racks.

'Here's one we thought we'd wear for the Wembley concert,' he said, lifting down a suit of black and white stripes with silver edgings. 'Bit naff, yeah?'

'Try it on,' she said, loving the way he appealed to her.

Unselfconsciously, he peeled his clothes off down to his boxer shorts. He caught her looking, embarrassed, at his perfect body. 'You should have seen me at your age.' He smiled wryly. 'A fifty kilo wimp you could have blown away with one breath. No girl would have been seen dead with me then.'

He burst into a little routine, softly singing, 'When I was young, my heart was yours . . .', their first big hit. It sent waves of nostalgia through Lucy. She began to dance, slowly, awkwardly, trying to mirror his movements.

Lek's arms stole around her. He felt cold and smooth. She could feel her heart thudding but though she was pressed against his bare chest she could feel nothing of his heartbeat.

'Have you got a girlfriend?' The words fell out of her mouth unbidden.

'All the girls are my girlfriend,' he murmured with a little smile.

He went on dancing, moving her slowly about the white room, skirting around the clothes that hung like silent witnesses.

'Lek,' she whispered, 'look at me. Like you did

before.' He looked, but now there was no flicker of recognition in his beautiful eyes. No light danced there. It was as if she was transparent.

She slipped out of his arms and felt a whiff of panic. Where was she? Why did she feel lost here?

'What do you think?' asked Lek. In a flash he had put on a leather jacket and black jeans, with a tie knotted loosely around his bare neck. Before she could say anything, he was changing again, this time into a blue knitted jerkin and white trousers. 'Or this?'

She shook her head uncertainly, but he took no notice.

'Or this?' – a beige suit with a high collar and a plum coloured shirt.

'Or this?' – torn denims and a black T-shirt with *Boyz* scrawled on it.

'Or this?'

He was moving so fast now, changing his appearance every few seconds, that he was becoming blurred. 'Stop it! Stop it, Lek!' shouted Lucy.

'What's the matter, Lucy?' he said softly, a smirk on his lips. He stepped up to her and ran a nail down her cheek. 'Don't you like all my disguises?'

'I want you . . . you . . .' she stuttered. 'As you are.'

That made him laugh aloud. It was a harsh laugh and the thin white walls of the room trembled.

'Stop it!' Lucy cried again.

He looked at her with narrowing eyes. 'What's

wrong with my little girl, then? My little fan, eh? Does she want to go home?'

Lucy felt revulsion. She turned and ran out of the room, down the parallel black lines. Then she stumbled away from them, seeking a way out. She blundered into one of the walls and found that it was made of paper. Her arm went through it. She tore a hole in it, but saw that the white spaces continued beyond it.

'Goodbye, Lucy,' she heard Lek call from a distance. 'Remember me.'

She stopped then, stood still, listened to the silence.

'Goodbye Lek,' she said at last.

Lucy was very quiet that evening. Her parents could not get much out of her, although she did reassure them that she had 'got what she wanted from the Replicator'. She was grateful when Gary rang.

Mum answered the phone. 'I'm not sure she's up to it, Gary,' she said, looking at Lucy's white, pinched face, the look of hurt in her eyes. But Lucy took the receiver.

'Hi, Gary,' she said. Gary sensed immediately by the tone of her voice, by the way she said those two words, that she wasn't going to brush him off this time.

She had taken Lek's picture down and had slid it inside a photo album dedicated to *Boyz*. The wall by her bed looked bare now. She felt bare too and was only too pleased when Gary, emboldened, suggested a date.

'How was the Dream Machine?' he asked tentatively; that's what he had dubbed the Replicator.

'Bit of a nightmare really,' Lucy answered with a laugh.

OFF-LINE

by Narinder Dhami

'You're not playing on that thing *again*?'

Andy fixed his eyes on the TV, where he was shooting his way expertly through level seven, and didn't say anything. That question was typical of his mum, he thought bitterly. He'd only put his Playstation on ten minutes ago, and she was making out he'd been on it for hours. Next she'd start going on about some newspaper article she'd seen recently about kids who spent all their time on their computers, and became social outcasts—

'I saw something in the papers this week about how many kids are becoming addicted to computers, especially to violent games.' His mum rustled briskly across the bedroom and pulled back the curtains Andy had carefully drawn to keep the sunlight off the TV

133

screen. He sighed inwardly, but didn't say anything. 'I'm surprised you've got any mates left, with the amount of time you spend up here on your own.'

'I've got plenty of mates.' Andy didn't usually bother arguing, but he was getting fed up with his mum only ever appearing when he was playing what was – OK, even he admitted it – a pretty mindless game. Sometimes, though, a mindless game was just what he needed, but his mum always seemed to be lurking around whenever he was kicking or punching or shooting some baddie on-screen. She never came in when he was surfing the Net looking for information for school projects, or when he was inputting his homework onto his Pentium and printing it out neatly on his laser printer, or when he was chatting to friends he'd made all over the world, like Miki in Tokyo or Jared in Oklahoma, or when he was e-mailing his dad. But maybe that was quite a good thing, anyway . . .

'Seriously, Andy, you've stopped doing all the things you used to do.' His mum had gone over to the doorway, and was standing there looking at him, her hands on her hips. 'I think you spend far too much time on that thing.' She nodded dismissively at his desk, crammed with hardware and software. 'You're getting addicted, like—'

She stopped. The words 'like your father' hung unspoken in the air between them, and Andy felt his insides clench. He had a feeling his mum had been working up to this for the last four months, ever since his dad had left. Things hadn't been right between them since then.

'I'm not addicted,' he muttered through gritted teeth.

'OK, prove it.' His mum gave him a challenging look. 'If you can keep off computers for a week, I'll buy you that mountain bike you asked me for six months ago.'

Andy blinked, and thought about that for a minute or two. He didn't care about the mountain bike much now – he hardly ever went out on the old bike he had at the moment – but he was suddenly determined to show his mum that he could do it. Somehow, it seemed important.

'OK,' he said, and gave his mum a defiant glance. His mum looked back at him a bit uncertainly, and Andy knew her well enough to guess that she was already beginning to wonder if she'd been a bit unfair, but he wasn't going to let her back out now. 'And if I do it, will you stop going on at me? About my computer, I mean?'

His mum hesitated, then nodded.

'It's a deal. Right, well, you'd better unplug all that stuff then and we'll put it downstairs in the living room.' She turned away. 'And it means no nipping round to Kevin's house to have a sneaky go on his machine – oh, and no visits to that Siberian café in the shopping mall.'

'Cyber café.' Andy grinned, and his mum smiled back.

'Whatever. I'm going downstairs to start the tea. Give me a shout when you're ready, and I'll help you carry everything down.'

Andy waited till he could hear his mum banging pots and pans around in the kitchen, then he switched his computer on. Quickly, he e-mailed his dad, telling him that he was going to be off-line for a week, but not to worry, that he would be in touch soon. His dad was a computer salesman and was probably away on a sales trip at the moment, but Andy knew that, wherever he was, his dad could pick up his e-mail through his new notebook computer and his mobile phone. At least that way they could keep in touch, even though he didn't see his dad much these days. Then he turned everything off again, and disconnected it all.

He carried his Playstation downstairs first, and took it into the living room. Even after four months, the large table in the corner still looked empty and forlorn. That was where Andy's dad had kept all his own computer equipment. It had covered the table, leaving no room for them to eat there, and it had been just one of the things that his mum and dad had argued about. Andy couldn't see the point of it, himself. They still had all their meals at the kitchen table, even now that dad and his computer had gone.

'I'll give you a hand.' His mum followed him back

upstairs, wiping her hands on a tea-towel. 'Let me carry the computer down, it's too heavy for you.'

Andy noted with resentment that she sounded cheerful. Too cheerful. Maybe his mum thought that this was her chance to break him of his computer habit for ever, he thought gloomily. Well, she was wrong. Computers were and always would be his number one hobby, but it wasn't as if he didn't do other things as well, was it? He played football, went to chess club at school, went to the cinema with his mates . . . His mum was being unfair, just because she hated computers. She only hated them because she refused to use them and so she didn't understand them, Andy thought resentfully. And because his dad had been – and still was – a workaholic.

'Right, that's that then.' His mum put the last box of disks onto the table, and dusted her hands off. 'Tea in ten minutes.' She headed for the kitchen, then hesitated in the doorway. 'There's a Humphrey Bogart film on tonight . . .' Andy's mum was a big fan of old black and white movies. 'Fancy watching it with me? We could make some popcorn.'

Andy shook his head.

'I've got homework to do.' His heart sank as he realized that now he was going to have to write his English essay out by hand instead of doing it on-screen. 'I think I'll make a start now.'

He didn't know for sure, Andy thought bitterly as he

climbed the stairs, but he'd bet any money that when people had started making movies in Hollywood, there'd been loads of fuss in the newspapers about how watching films was going to turn kids wild, and stop them from studying. Nothing much had changed, except that now it was computers that grown-ups like his mum were going on about. Not for much longer though – Andy's face split into a big grin. All he had to do was be a computer-free zone for the next week, and then his mum would have to stop her nagging for ever. Simple.

'I've seen that look somewhere before,' Kevin Simpson said thoughtfully.

'What?' Andy blinked at his friend. He'd been sitting staring across the classroom at the computer in the corner, where Lucy Ross and Kavita Patel were bent over the keyboard, writing a story. Andy couldn't even see the screen from where he was sitting, but he just couldn't help staring.

'I said, I've seen that look somewhere before.' Kevin snapped his fingers. 'Got it! That's just how my dad looked when he gave up smoking. If he saw anyone else with a cigarette, he'd stare at them just like you're staring at that computer.'

'Ha ha. Very funny.' Andy looked down at his maths book. It was now Thursday, three days since the bet with his mum had started. Three whole days without even touching a keyboard. And there were still four days to go. He wasn't sure he was going to make it.

'Kev—' he said tentatively.

'No.' Kevin was already shaking his head. 'Your mum told mine about the bet when she met her in Sainsbury's last night. My mum'd skin me alive if I let you have a go on my machine.'

Andy chewed the end of his pencil, then gave his friend an evil grin.

'I think we're down on the computer list for tomorrow,' he said. 'I don't think using the computer at school counts, does it? I mean, that's *education*.'

'Well, that's certainly what we're here for, but there's not much of it going on at the moment.' Miss Carpenter, their teacher, materialized suddenly behind Kevin, and gave Andy's empty page a pointed look. 'By the way, Andy, I met your mum at the supermarket last night. She mentioned that you were giving up computers for a week . . .' Miss Carpenter leaned over and ticked Kevin's sums. 'So I've crossed you off the computer list for tomorrow.'

'Teachers!' Andy said bitterly when Miss Carpenter had gone away to pounce on somebody else. 'What was she doing in Sainsbury's anyway?'

'Even teachers have to eat.' Kevin shrugged. 'You coming to football practice after school then?'

Andy opened his mouth to say no, then wondered what he was going to do if he didn't. He'd probably go home and sit and stare at his blank computer screen like a very sad person. Anything was better than that.

'OK . . .'

'Oh, aren't we the lucky ones!' boomed Mr Bryan, the games teacher, sarcastically, when Andy turned up for football practice with Kevin later that day. 'Andrew Kirby's back to show us how the game of football should be played.'

'Yes, sir,' Andy said politely. Mr Bryan's sarcasm was legendary throughout the school, and it was best just to let him get on with it. Unless you had a burning desire to get your head chewed off, that is.

'Well, after taking four months off, you should be about as fit as a tortoise with arthritis.' Mr Bryan hurled a football at Andy, who just managed to catch it before it blasted a hole in his stomach. 'Come on, let's get started.'

They spent the next ten minutes dribbling round cones, but Andy kept losing his ball because he couldn't concentrate. Four months? Was it *really* four months since he'd last been to football practice? He couldn't believe it. Or was it just Bryan being extra-sarcastic? Andy began counting back the days in his head, and ended up almost impaling himself on a plastic cone. It *was* four months, give or take a few days.

'Take no notice of old Bryan,' Kevin said when they went to change at the end of the practice. 'He's just a bit narked because he thought you were going to be one of his star players.'

'What're you talking about?' Andy said, amazed, and then an ancient memory flickered into his mind. Mr Bryan, for once not being sarcastic, telling him about six months ago that he'd be a decent player if he went to the practices regularly . . .

It was the same when he went to chess club with Kevin the following lunch-time. Mrs O'Connor, the teacher who ran the club, wasn't quite as sarcastic as Mr Bryan, but she wasn't far off.

'Oh, so you're back, Andy,' she said, looking at him over the top of her glasses. 'We could have done with a player like you when we entered the Inter-Schools Chess Tournament last month.'

'Did you win, miss?' Andy asked politely. He couldn't remember hearing anything about how the team had got on.

'We lost in the first round,' Mrs O'Connor said bitterly. 'Well, we'd better find you a beginner to play against. You're probably a bit rusty after four months away.'

'It's OK, miss.' Andy frowned. He hadn't been to chess club for four months? He was sure it hadn't been as long as that. 'I'll play against Kev, like I usually do.'

Mrs O'Connor smiled.

'Good luck.'

As he sat across the chess board from Kevin, Andy

silently worked out dates and times in his head. It *was* four months since he'd last been to chess club. He was so busy being amazed by this that he didn't notice that Kevin had checkmated him. Twice.

'Sorry,' Kevin said apologetically. 'I've been practising over the last few months.'

'It's OK.' Andy's head was spinning. He was almost starting to wonder if his mum had a point . . .

'How long is it since we went to that Saturday club at the pictures?' he asked Kevin carefully later that day. School was over, and they were round at Andy's house, working on his old bike. Kevin had suggested that they take their bikes over to the park that evening, and Andy had agreed, until he'd found out that he had two flat tyres.

Kevin shrugged.

'Oh, a couple of months.'

'Oh.' That wasn't too bad.

'Well, maybe three or four.' Kevin nodded. 'Yep, about four months ago.'

Andy bit his lip. Much as he hated to admit it, he was beginning to see that his mum was right. For the last four months at least, he'd done hardly anything except stay inside with his computer.

'Want to go this week?'

'Sure,' Kevin said easily. 'But I thought you went to stay with your dad at weekends.'

Andy felt a sharp pain hit him right in the middle of his

stomach. It was so long since he'd talked about his dad to anyone, it gave him a jolt to hear Kevin mention him.

'Not this weekend,' he said slowly. 'He's away on a sales trip.'

'Oh.' Kevin began to pump up Andy's back tyre. 'You don't see him much, do you?'

'No.' Andy worked it out quickly in his head. He was supposed to go and stay with his dad every second weekend, but he hadn't been over there for over a month because his dad was either away or he was working at home. And maybe that was why he'd been so wrapped up in his computer for the last few months, Andy thought with a sudden flash of insight, because it made him feel closer to his dad . . .

'Have a good ride?' his mum asked him when Andy got home from the park.

'Yeah.' Andy had forgotten what a good laugh he'd always had with Kevin when they went out on their bikes. At least they'd managed to stay mates, he thought guiltily, even though they hadn't done much except play computer games together occasionally for the last four months.

His mum smiled triumphantly.

'See?' she said. 'I knew you'd realize you were missing out because you spent so much time on that awful machine. Get some plates out for me, would you?'

Andy opened his mouth to protest, then closed it

again. His mum *had* been right – sort of. But that wasn't the whole story . . . He wasn't going to pretend that he'd lost interest in computers, just to make her feel better about his dad leaving. He still loved computers and he always would, regardless of his dad. But he was beginning to realize that he and his mum still had a lot of talking to do, and that making that silly bet hadn't really solved anything. The other thing he realized he had to do was to contact his dad, and tell him that he wanted to see him. Soon. And that they had to sort out a rota for visiting and stick to it, never mind his work. He didn't want to phone, because his dad never had time to talk. But if he e-mailed him, then his dad would have to take notice of it. Unfortunately, there were still three days of the bet left to go . . .

With so much going on in his head, Andy couldn't sleep that night. He'd spent ages working out what he was going to e-mail to his dad, and now it kept replaying itself over and over in his mind like a tape recorder. After dozing and waking up again for hours, he finally sat up in bed, and looked at his watch. Two a.m. He was going to be zonked out at school tomorrow, he thought grimly, but maybe, just maybe, he could sneak downstairs and quietly e-mail his dad while his mum was asleep. His mum hadn't been sleeping well for the last few months, and quite often she stayed up watching old movies on the cable channels until early into the morning, but Andy was sure she'd gone to bed by now

because he couldn't hear the faint hum of the TV. If he was quiet, she wouldn't hear him . . .

Andy crept out of his room. His mum's bedroom door was shut, and he hesitated, wondering whether she was in bed or not, but not daring to open it and find out. He found out, though, when he was half-way down the stairs. The living-room door was slightly ajar, and the light from the TV was shining through the gap. Except that Andy could see from where he was standing that the TV was switched off.

He went downstairs, and pushed the door open wider. His mum was sitting at the table, bent over his computer. Somehow she'd managed to access the Internet, and was avidly reading a Web site on old Judy Garland films.

Andy gasped. His mum heard, and looked round. She began to blush a bright, embarrassed red, and went on blushing. Neither of them spoke for a moment or two.

'I couldn't sleep,' his mum said at last.

'Me neither,' Andy said truthfully.

'About that bet—' they both said together, and then they laughed.

'Never mind that wretched bet.' His mum held her hand out to him. 'Is there any stuff about Humphrey Bogart on here?'

'Let's have a look.' Andy slid into the chair beside her, and he knew that from now on everything was going to be all right

146

THE WEATHER MAN

by Helen Dunmore

Dad should never have taken it on. As the day of the fair came closer and closer his face crumpled up with worry. One night I woke at three a.m. and wanted some cornflakes, so I crept down to the kitchen. The light was on and there was Dad sitting at the table, adding up columns of figures. Dad was Chair of the Grand Summer Fair Committee, and what he did was worry. He worried when the entrance tickets came back printed upside down. He worried in case Jem Wheeler superglued the coconuts onto the coconut-shy again. He worried because three different ice-cream vans wanted to drive onto the field and there was only room for one. Dad worried about everything. The fair's a big thing in our village, and it raises loads of money. Everybody does something. Even the little kids have drinks stalls and sell cup-cakes their mums have made. We have jugglers and gymnastics displays and go-karting with bales of straw round the track, and fancy dress and a beer tent. You can guess the weight of a pig and win twenty pounds. For a pound you get in the tea-tent, with all the cakes you can eat. Lots of people come just for the cakes.

Dad had his head in his hands. I poured sugar and milk onto my cornflakes and sat down at the table. He didn't even notice, let alone tell me to go to bed.

'You OK, Dad?'

Dad groaned. Then he sat up and stared wildly around the kitchen. 'Listen to it! Just listen to it!' he said.

'What?'

'The rain, of course.'

'Oh.' Mum and I had been trying to keep the word 'rain' out of the house. We knew how depressed Dad was getting. It had been raining for twenty-one days, and there was only a week to go until the fair. The sky looked as if it could go on pouring out rain for ever. Thick, heavy, cold rain. The field where the fair was held every year was a soggy quagmire. 'We can't put that pig into it. It'll drown,' said Dad gloomily.

'It's got to stop raining some time,' I said encouragingly, and put an extra spoonful of sugar onto my cornflakes.

'I should have got weather insurance,' said Dad. 'It's all my fault. Just because it was so hot last summer, I thought it'd be the same this year. What if we can't hold the fair at all? What if I have to tell everyone it's been cancelled, and we've got no insurance?'

'It's not your fault, Dad. You can't help the rain.'

'I should have known,' said Dad, and put his head back in his hands. 'The Committee'll blame me, and I don't blame them.'

I wished Mum was there. She was better at cheering Dad up than I was. Then I thought of what Dad had said. 'Can't you still get it, Dad? Weather insurance, I mean?'

'It's too late. The premiums'll be sky-high with all this rain. And another deepening trough of low pressure coming in from the Atlantic, it said on the weather forecast.'

'Have you tried?'

Dad said nothing. I knew that meant he hadn't. 'We could have a look in the *Yellow Pages*,' I suggested.

'Oh yes! Of course! The *Yellow Pages*!' said Dad sarcastically. 'I'm sure we'll find the answer to everything in there.'

I said nothing. I took the *Yellow Pages* off the shelf and began to flip through it. I was feeling wide awake now. I looked under 'Insurance' first. Nothing. Just insurance for houses and cars. Then I turned to 'Weather', and ran my finger down the entry, and there it was. I pushed the book under Dad's nose, triumphantly.

'There you are, Dad. "John Smith's Computerized Total Weather Assurance Service".'

'*John Smith*. Sounds like an alias to me,' said Dad, but he took his head out of his hands and read the entry.

'Does "assurance" mean the same as "insurance"?' I asked. I could tell Dad didn't really know, because he just mumbled something. Then he stood up, keeping his finger on the entry, and grabbed the phone with his other hand.

'Dad.'

'What?'

'It's three o'clock in the morning.'

'Oh.'

The rain drummed on the windows. Dad sighed, and I poured out some more cornflakes.

When I came back from school, Dad was already home.

'Your dad's finished work early,' said Mum. 'He wants you to go out with him. Something to do with the fair. Have you got any homework?'

'No.' Behind her back I could see Dad signalling. The minute we were outside he said, 'I didn't want to worry your mother.'

'What do you mean?'

Dad looked guilty. 'She thinks I've already got weather insurance.'

'Dad! Did you tell her that?'

''Course I didn't. Not exactly. But there's no point both of us getting in a state, is there?'

'Hmm,' I said.

'And he sounds very good, I must say. John Smith. That's where we're going,' said Dad, as if I hadn't guessed.

'Can he give you insurance?'

'We've got to meet him. Give him the details. Talk it over and he'll give us a quote.'

John Smith's Computerized Total Weather Assurance Service was based in Beckhampton, six miles away. I was expecting an office, with a receptionist and a waiting-room, but Dad turned into a shabby little street by the canal.

'Fore Street. Good, this must be it.'

We stopped by the shabbiest house of all. The gate hung off its hinges and the door paint was so blistered you could have pulled it off in strips. There was water pouring out of a broken roof gutter. Dad had the big umbrella and he held it over both of us while he rang the bell. I could tell from the house what John Smith was going to be like.

But he wasn't. John Smith wasn't old and sad and shabby. He wore jeans and trainers and a dark-blue T-shirt and he was even taller than my dad. His smile was easy and friendly.

'Come in,' he said. The hall was bright after the rainy street. 'This way.' We followed him into a room with a red carpet, white walls, and three black, soft chairs. Nothing else. Not a computer screen to be seen. We all sat down. Dad and I looked expectantly at John Smith, and he looked back at us as if he expected something too. The easy smile was still there, but his eyes were sharp.

'Right,' he said at last. 'What kind of weather do you want?'

Dad looked at him as if he was mad.

'What do you mean, what kind of weather? I'm running a summer fair in the middle of a field. I want sun, of course.'

'Ah, yes,' said John Smith. 'Of course you do. But there's sun, and sun. Do you want a breezy day, with sun and a bit of cloud in it, looking as if it might rain towards night?'

At the word 'rain', Dad shuddered. 'No,' he said, 'just sun.'

'Or do you want a real scorcher, the kind of day you get in the middle of a heatwave? People with sunstroke in the St John's Ambulance tent? Refrigeration systems breaking down?'

'That sounds a bit much,' said Dad.

'OK. We're getting there. What I believe you want is a perfect English summer day. Little wisps of white cloud in the morning, then clear skies all day. Hot, but not too hot. You want the sound of a cricket match going on in the distance, am I right? Picnics in the shade. Ice clinking in glasses.'

'We don't play cricket at the fair,' said Dad, 'but the rest of it would do fine.'

John Smith sounded just as if he was ordering weather for us from a catalogue. He took a pad of paper and a black pen and began to write. Then he said, 'It's weather *assurance* I'm offering, you understand, not weather *insurance*.'

'What's the difference?' I asked.

'Weather insurance *insures* you, in case you don't get the weather you want. Weather assurance *assures* you that you will get the weather you want.'

'But it can't,' I said. 'Nobody can guarantee what the weather's going to be like.'

Dad frowned at me. John Smith flicked me a look, and said smoothly, 'I think we've talked long enough. Let me show you the technology.'

The technology was amazing. The computers must have been worth thousands of pounds. Maybe even tens of thousands. Words like 'state-of-the-art' floated in my mind as I stared at the gleaming banks of screens and keyboards. John Smith crossed to one of the screens, sat down, and began to type on the keyboard.

'I'm just putting your requirements in here.' Dad and I looked at each other. John Smith finished typing and pressed 'return'. Then he pulled down the control panel menu. 'It'll start its search now. It's pretty quick. I upgraded the find-program last week.' We watched as the computer worked. About eight seconds later the 'ready' box on the right side of the screen began to pulse.

'Great. We'll go in and take a look,' said John Smith, and he double-clicked the box.

I've never seen a computer download visuals as fast as that one. The screen swam for a second, then steadied. I moved forward.

'Want to sit here?' asked John Smith, getting up. I sat down. He took a pair of headphones, and fitted them over my ears. My head filled with the sound of summer. A lazy zing of bees. Laughter in the distance. The thwack of a ball on a bat, then a shout. On the screen, the leaves of a huge oak quivered. People were picnicking in its shade, watching the cricket match. There was a boy about my age, lying on his back in the grass, staring straight up into the perfect blue sky. He could have been me except for the clothes he was wearing. They were all wearing old-fashioned clothes. Even the little girls had petticoats down to their ankle boots. The cricket clothes were white, but the style was different. Their pads looked heavy and clumsy. I watched closely as the bowler ran up and the batsman hit the ball out towards the boundary. The style was different. It wasn't quite like the cricket I was used to.

I could hear the buzz of voices through my head-phones but I couldn't make out what they were saying. I had the strangest feeling, as if I had only to reach out my hand to feel that soft green grass, and the sun on my arms, and the little breeze that stirred the leaves. I must have moved forward, because John Smith said quite

sharply, 'Don't,' and he took the headphones off me. Dad was looking at the screen too, but he hadn't got his reading glasses with him. He wouldn't be seeing any of the detail, just a blur of green and blue. 'Looks good,' he said. 'If that's what your assurance can come up with, count me in.'

I stared at John Smith. 'How do you do it?' I asked.

'Storage and retrieval of information, that's all,' he said coolly. 'That's what these computers are for. I've got hundreds of years stored up in this room. Something to match every client's requirements. You tell me you want a summer day. Then tell me what kind of summer day, and I can find it for you. It'll be in here somewhere. The program will keep on searching until it achieves compatibility. And I think you'll agree it's achieved compatibility here.'

'It certainly has,' said Dad happily.

'What if we'd said we wanted a storm?' I asked. John Smith looked at me, a long look. 'You're an awkward customer, aren't you?' he said. He cleared the screen, and began to type in more information. He was right, the find-program was incredibly quick. A few seconds later I saw it. A sea knocked into great lumps by the punches of the wind. Beach huts whirling then splintering to matchwood. Trees torn up by their roots. Panels of glass sucked in by giant breath. 'Put the headphones on again,' said John Smith. I didn't want to, but I wasn't going to say no. I put them on. There was a long continuous howl like an express train circling my head. It didn't stop. I shivered and pulled off the headphones. 'The night of 15 October 1987,' said John Smith. 'Is that what you want? It's all in there. All stored. Every bit of information. It can be yours any time you want.'

Dad was getting impatient. 'We don't want storms,' he said.

But I was still looking at John Smith. 'You mean what you've got stored in there can come out of the computer into the real world? Is that how Weather Assurance works?'

'Computerized Total Weather Assurance,' John Smith corrected me. 'Real world? What do you mean by real world? Are you sure you can tell the difference between reality and virtual reality? What is reality anyway?'

I remembered the express-train howl of the hurricane, and the soft murmur of summer bees. I wasn't sure. It was fantastic, and a bit frightening too. And there was something a bit frightening in the way John Smith was looking at us. It was a hungry look, as if he needed us much, much more than we needed him.

'So can you guarantee us sunshine?' Dad was sticking to the point.

John Smith smiled. 'I have so many days,' he said. 'I have so much weather. All waiting for a chance to come out again. Sunshine? Of course. You shall have that very day you saw on the screen.'

Dad smiled back. 'Sounds great to me. Where do I write the cheque?'

I made myself smile too, but there was something niggling in the back of my mind. Something we'd done in history. Somewhere I'd seen pictures of people who looked just like the people on screen. A perfect summer day. The last perfect summer before . . . before what? What had happened next? *And what would happen if that day got its chance to come out again, into the real world?*

'Can I see the screen again?' I asked. 'That summer day looked so fantastic. I want to see what our day's going to be like.'

John Smith looked at us both. 'You've decided, then,' he said. 'Good. I'll just set up the screen again, then I'll go and arrange the paperwork.'

The summer day floated on screen again. The kind of summer day everyone dreams about. Perfect peace. I looked at the clothes again. The women's skins were pale, as if they never sunbathed. Suddenly a boy on a bicycle appeared on the dusty road beside the field. He was cycling hard, waving. He shouted, as if he had a message for the cricketers and the people sitting under the oak tree. But they hadn't turned round. They hadn't seen him yet. Their summer day went on.

'When was it?' I asked casually. 'Have you got a date for this day, like you have for the hurricane?'

'Of course. Every day has a date. It couldn't be stored otherwise. Let me see. That one's easy. 28 August

1914. I'll go and do that paperwork and I'll be right back.'

Dad was smiling. He hadn't been listening to anything I'd said. All he cared about was getting John Smith's Computerized Total Weather Assurance Service, and solving the problem of the fair. He didn't want to know any more. I didn't know what to do. I could hear John Smith going downstairs, but he'd be back soon.

'Dad,' I said urgently, 'what happened on 28 August 1914?'

'August 1914? Wasn't that the start of the First World War? Seem to remember that one. Look at the sun on those leaves. Just think, if we get a day like that for the fair . . .'

He was right. Of course. The day looked so peaceful, but it wasn't really. Those people didn't know it, but their whole world was about to change. What happened to that boy lying on his back in the grass? And what was going to happen if we let that day out into the real world again? I shivered. It was all too dangerous. That day had got to stay in the past where it belonged, where it couldn't do any more harm. But I couldn't explain it all to Dad, not in the time it'd take John Smith to sort out the paperwork and come back upstairs.

'The thing is, Dad,' I said, 'I think he's only showing us part of the picture.'

'What? What do you mean?' The happy smile faded from Dad's face. He looked worried again.

'I think something's just about to go wrong. Look at those clouds in the corner of the screen.'

Dad peered, but of course he couldn't see without his reading glasses.

'Big purple clouds,' I said.

'Oh no!' said Dad. 'Storm clouds!'

'Yeah. Wait a minute, let me listen.' I put on the headphones again. I frowned. 'Dad, this is awful. I can hear thunder. It's a long way off but it's getting closer.'

'I can't believe it. Why didn't he tell us?'

'Because we might have said no. He wants to sell us the day.'

'I knew it was too good to be true,' said Dad. He put his head in his hands. 'Let's get out of here.'

We met John Smith at the top of the stairs. His smooth smile faded as he saw our faces. Dad was embarrassed, but firm. 'I'm sorry,' he said, 'but I've had time to think and I've changed my mind. I'm just going to have to take a chance on the weather. Better the devil you know.' John Smith started. Was it my imagination, or did he go a little paler?

'Take a chance? You'll never get a chance like this again,' he said. His voice clutched at us. He shot me a look as if he knew I was the one who'd spoiled everything for him. 'Let me take you through it again,' he urged Dad.

But he didn't know Dad. Once he changes his mind, that's it. 'Better the devil you know,' Dad repeated. 'And now we'll have to be getting along. I'm sorry to have taken up your time.'

Suddenly, John Smith looked huge, blocking the way to the front door. My heart bumped. Was he going to keep us here and only let us go once we'd agreed to take 28 August 1914 with us? No-one knew where we were, even Mum. But Dad didn't seem to notice the thunderous look on John Smith's face. Maybe he couldn't see it without his reading glasses.

'Excuse me,' he said, politely but firmly. I didn't see John Smith step aside, but he seemed suddenly smaller. And then we were out of the house, in the rain. I never thought I'd be so pleased to hear the sound of rain falling on Dad's big umbrella.

I thought Dad would be gloomy right up to the day of the fair, but he wasn't. Our visit to John Smith seemed to have cheered him up. He said things like, 'We can always put plenty of straw under the pig,' and, 'Well, they've all got umbrellas, haven't they?'

The day of the fair came. It was a bit rainy, then a bit sunny, then rainy again. People came with boots and umbrellas and the pig looked quite comfortable on layers of straw. I was glad it was like that. I didn't really want that perfect summer day from long ago, now that I knew how it ended. Since we came back from John Smith's Computerized Total Weather Assurance

Service I'd read about the First World War in Dad's encyclopaedia, and I didn't like the sound of it. I wouldn't have liked to be that boy under the tree. I was glad those faraway terrible things weren't going to get a chance to come alive again.

There's one more thing. I guessed the weight of the pig and got it dead right. I won twenty pounds.

ARTIFICIAL INTELLIGENCE

by Malorie Blackman

'Come on, Mum, you *must* know.'

'Claire, how many more times?' Mum said, exasperated. 'I don't know what your dad is working on. You know he doesn't like to show us what he's doing until it's completely finished and he's totally happy with it.'

'But what d'you think it might be?' I persisted. 'I mean, why did he need all that information from me? And why did he scan my mind for my brain patterns? What's that got to do with . . . ?'

'Claire, read my lips – I DON'T KNOW.' Mum raised an impatient, grey hand to swot away an irritating bluebottle. She made contact and it fell dead at her feet.

I decided not to push it. From the sparks practically

flying out of Mum's eyes, it was obvious she was beginning to get more than annoyed.

'Your dad said he'd show us what he's been working on later today and he will. Until then you'll just have to wait,' Mum said, calming down slightly. She picked up the fly and dropped it into the bin by her armchair.

I stood up.

'Where're you going?' Mum asked.

'To do my homework.'

'To do your homework or to play on the Cybanet?' Mum asked drily.

'I don't *play* on the Cybanet. I work, I research, I gather data, I further my education . . .'

'But mostly you play!' laughed Mum.

I couldn't help laughing as well – because it was true!

'I'm not going to play now though. I'm going to talk to my pen pal,' I said.

'You've found one at last, have you?'

'Mum, where've you been? I've had a pen pal for three weeks now. Her name is Gail. And we've got so many things in common. It's amazing.'

'What about all the other people who e-mailed you?' Mum asked.

'It's all right. I told them that I've found a pen pal and I only want one for the time being.'

'I hope you were polite.'

'Aren't I always?!' I replied.

I ran up to my bedroom, ignoring Mum's guffaws behind me. Switching on my computer, I waited for the system to boot up. I couldn't wait to talk to Gail again. To tell the truth I don't have many friends. Most of the kids in my class think I'm a bit stand-offish. They think I fancy myself. I don't. I really don't. I'm just a bit shy. But *everyone* has heard of my dad and they think that because he's famous, I think I'm too good for them. That couldn't be further from the truth either, but no-one in my class has stuck around long enough to find out. I mean, I'm proud of my dad, I really am. It's just that he cares more about his work than he does about Mum and me. Mum says that's normal and to be expected and I'll understand when I grow up. Somehow I doubt that. Dad's away in his lab as often as he can manage it. I've heard Mum and Dad discussing it so often now. I've lost count of the times I've wished they'd have a shouting, screaming quarrel about it. At least that would be more *real*. But they say shouting and screaming and behaving that way is for children, not adults. And then they say, 'Never mind, Claire, you'll grow out of it.'

To be honest, I'm not sure I want to.

At last the PC was ready to use. I started up the Cybanet link and input my user name and password. Then I selected the option to create a message and started typing:

To: Gail@gailmail.private.uk
From: Claire@clairemail.private.uk

Hi Gail,
How are you? Dad still hasn't told
us what he's working on. The
minute I know, I'll be straight on
the computer to you! Dad always
swears Mum and me to secrecy but
you're almost like my sister, so I
can tell you. I know you won't
tell anyone else. Abletech, the
computer company Dad works for,
are really excited about this
latest invention - at least that's
what Dad says. I'm not surprised
you've heard of my dad - everyone
has. He's a computer genius - at
least, that's what the papers say.
And Dad says he's working on
something that will make modern
day computers seem like 'stone age
tools' - his words, not mine. I
hope your dad pays more attention
to you than mine does to me. Get
typing. I'm waiting. Your friend,
Claire.

I sent off the message, hoping Gail would be at her PC
so I'd get a message straight back. I was in luck. I didn't
have long to wait.

To: Claire@clairemail.private.uk
From: Gail@gailmail.private.uk

Hi, Claire,
It's great to hear from you again.
I'm glad about what you said. To
be honest, I already think of you
as a sister. You talk about your
father as if you don't like him
very much, but I envy you. I'd
love a family, a real family, any
kind of family. That's why it's
wonderful that you want us to be
as close as sisters. I live in one
room that I'm meant to call home
but it isn't - not really. My
father looks after me but it's not
because he cares about me, about
who I am *inside*. He just looks
after me because he hopes that
some day, I'll make him rich. I've
heard him talking to his friends
about me. They all talk in front
of me as if I'm not there, or as
if I'm deaf. I bet your father
isn't like that. Write soon. Love,
Gail.

I frowned at the screen as I reread Gail's message. I was just about to start typing again, when Mum yelled from the kitchen, 'Claire, your dad's just been on the phone.

He's at the lab and he wants us to come over as soon as possible. He's ready to show us what he's been working on.'

I ran out of the bedroom. Gail was forgotten.

'You mean we're actually going to see what he's been doing for the last year?' I couldn't believe my ears. And strangely enough, even though I resented all the time Dad had spent away from us working on his new project, I still couldn't wait to see it.

'Grab your coat.' Mum sighed, wiping her hands. 'And remember to look suitably impressed.'

'I present the next stage in the computer technology revolution,' Dad announced. 'Come on out, AI-2!'

It walked into the room and stood next to Dad.

'Well? What do you think?' Dad asked, eagerly.

I eyed Dad's latest invention with a growing sense of revulsion. I couldn't help it. It was *grotesque*. Like nothing I'd ever seen before. It was shorter than me and rounder and with two more arms it could've been some kind of nasty, giant insect.

'What's wrong with it?' The beaming smile on Dad's face vanished, like a torch being switched off.

I glanced at Mum. She frowned at me.

'I . . . nothing.' But it was too late. Dad had already read my expression.

'Come on, Claire. Tell me what's wrong with it.' Dad's voice was cold, defensive.

'Why does it look like that?' I asked.

'Like what?'

'So . . . so strange-looking.'

'Ah! Now that's quite interesting.' Dad rubbed his hands together with glee. 'I and my colleagues believe that computer technology in its current form has gone as far as it can. We believe a brand-new approach is called for, so we got permission to experiment on some DNA from the Natural History Museum. We managed to get some DNA samples that were over four thousand years old. Imagine that! Four thousand years old! And after years of false starts we managed to rebuild the DNA sequences and start some cell cultures using other primates to fill in the missing data. And from those first simple cells we have developed what you see here.'

Dad did everything but bow when he'd finished speaking. He reminded me of a preening peacock. I walked up to it and prodded it with my finger. It felt like nothing I'd ever touched before.

'Why does it look so . . . so *horrible*?' I couldn't help it. I had to say the word.

'What do you mean? It's meant to be *you*!' Dad's smile broadened. 'I modelled her face on yours.'

I stared at him. He must have lost his mind. This . . . this *thing* standing in front of me was meant to be *me*? What an insult!

'Obviously not exactly you, but she's based on you.'

'I don't understand.' I wasn't sure I wanted to understand.

'I scanned your brain patterns as the blueprint for her synaptic pathways. She's the prototype for the next generation of computers. I wanted her to be able to reason things out for herself – to have true artificial intelligence. Left to her own devices she might have had limited intelligence but I decided it would be beneficial to imprint your brain patterns into her processor. And I was right.'

'You really used my brain patterns on it?' I was appalled.

'Remember a couple of months ago when I recorded some of your memories on the cogno-chip? Well, I used the information from that chip on AI-2.'

'AI-2?' Mum chipped in.

'Artificial Intelligence – second prototype: AI-2 for short,' Dad said proudly.

This was getting worse and worse. AI-2 stood in front of me on two artificial legs, and its lips were turned up in what I can only assume was an attempt at a smile.

'Gordon, why does it look so . . . so *peculiar*?' Mum asked.

'Well, she's made of a new kind of material – like nothing we've ever seen before. And I found that the more she learnt and analysed, the more her central processor *grew*. Imagine that! It actually increased in weight and mass. It was completely unexpected. But the material used to house the processor grows with it, as and when necessary,' Dad explained. 'Her processor is a brand-new design, like nothing anyone's ever seen before. Unlike us, her processor sends both electrical and chemical signals. Each instruction is a mixture of both. Isn't that fantastic! Think of the built-in redundancy, think of the routing mechanism with its automatic backups! She's moved beyond even my wildest expectations . . .'

I faded out at that point. I just stared at AI-2. It stared back at me.

'So, Claire, what d'you think?'

I only faded in again when Dad said my name.

'That thing's really got my memories?' I frowned.

Dad had well and truly lost his mind. How could he? Especially without my permission. *How could he?*

'Only up until three months ago. The two of you diverged from then,' Dad added, defensively. 'I didn't think you'd mind.'

We both knew he was lying. He knew exactly how I'd feel, he'd just decided to go ahead anyway, figuring that once it was done, there wouldn't be much I could do about it. The same old story. It wasn't the first time and it wouldn't be the last.

'Is that all I am to you? A source of material for your experiments?' I asked.

'Now, Claire, you're behaving like a child again.'

Dad brushed my accusation aside. He didn't even bother to deny it.

'I am a child – remember?' I told him.

'Well, thank goodness AI-2 is more level-headed than you,' Dad said, a sharp edge to his voice. 'Say hello to my daughter, AI-2.'

'Hello, Claire.' Even AI-2's voice sounded strange. It wasn't like a normal voice at all. It was echoey and breathy. 'I've been looking forward to meeting you.'

I still couldn't believe it. Dad had built a free-standing, fully automated computer with my brain patterns and what was meant to be my face. If I really looked like AI-2, I'd walk around with a paper bag on my head.

'I don't like it, Dad. When are you going to de-activate it?'

'Deactivate AI-2!' Dad was aghast. 'I've worked for years to perfect her and you want me to destroy her?'

'Dad, it's not real,' I tried to argue.

'Not real! She's as real as you or I. And she's a "she", not an "it"!' Dad was practically shouting at me by now. 'AI-2 can think for herself. I don't mean follow predefined decisions already laid out in a program. I mean she can really think for herself. Analyse, reason, learn. I've even put a PC in her room with lots of learning software and a connection to the Cybanet so that she can watch and listen and learn about our world at her own pace – but she's ahead of us already.'

'Mum, do something. Make him switch it off. Make him get rid of it,' I appealed.

Mum stared at AI-2 and just shook her head.

'Claire, I really don't understand your attitude.' Dad glared at me, but I didn't care.

It was as if I'd asked him to get rid of . . . well, get rid of me. No, I take that back. He wouldn't have raised as much fuss if it was only me he had to get rid of. Dad was given me. The AI-2, he'd had to make.

'Please, Claire.' AI-2 smiled again. 'I am your friend. And you will always come first with Gordon.'

'Don't call my dad that,' I said, stung.

'I told her to call me Gordon.' Dad sprang to her defence. 'What else is she going to call me? Claire, if you can't be happy for me, you can leave. Go on. And I'll tell you something else, if the AI-2 were in your shoes and your roles were reversed, she wouldn't be making all this fuss.'

I couldn't take any more. I really couldn't. I mustered up the filthiest look I could and sent it hurtling towards Dad. Then I ran out of the lab.

Minutes later, Mum joined me in our car. She drove us home. We both sat in stony silence. As soon as we got home, I tried to run up to my room but Mum stopped me.

'Claire, I want to talk to you.'

'I don't want to talk to you or anyone.'

173

'Tough!' Mum pulled then pushed me into the living room. 'Sit down.'

I sat down, suddenly and inexplicably sad, tired. Mum put her arm around my shoulders and sighed.

'Claire, you're not as tough as you like to think you are,' she said. 'And just because your father can be a bit thoughtless sometimes, that doesn't mean that you have to follow in his footsteps.'

'What d'you mean?' I sniffed.

'You were a bit . . . abrupt.' Mum chose her words carefully. 'I know it was hard to hide what you really felt, especially when that computer monstrosity was just launched at us out of the blue like that, but you have to learn to keep quiet until you can control exactly what you want to say and how you're going to say it.'

'Like you do?'

Mum sighed again. 'Like I do. I had to learn and so will you. That's what sets us apart from any other species. Our ability to think dispassionately. When you've learnt to control your responses then you're truly an adult. When you've learnt to suppress your feelings until you no longer have them, then you've arrived.'

'Don't you have any feelings at all?' I asked Mum.

She shook her head.

Not even for me? I wanted to ask, but somehow the words wouldn't come.

'Will I be like you one day?' I asked instead.

'Of course!'

'What about . . . what about when you have children?' I whispered.

'You're my daughter, Claire. Nothing will change that.'

It wasn't the answer I was hoping for, but I could see that it would have to do.

'In the meantime, Claire, you have to remember that you're Gordon's daughter as well, and treat him accordingly,' Mum continued.

'But why? Why can't I tell Dad exactly how I feel? He had no right to use me as his guinea pig.'

'I agree. But there are ways of saying these things. And as they say, you catch more flies with honey than with vinegar.'

I went up to my room, thinking about what Mum had said. I connected up to the Cybanet. Although I knew Mum was right, I couldn't calm down. There was a strange kind of anger inside of me, not burning hot, but burning cold, trickling its way through my body like liquid nitrogen.

```
To:Gail@gailmail.private.uk
From: Claire@clairemail.private.uk

Hello Gail,
I'm sorry I didn't reply to your
last message right away but
something came up. My dad, the
```

so-called genius, has invented what he calls the next step in computing. He's built a fully operational, totally automated computer capable of true artificial intelligence. But he's a liar. He hasn't created a computer capable of AI. All he did was copy my brain patterns into his contraption and use my mind as the basis for its thoughts. Mum and I went to see it today. It was horrible. It had two legs and two arms like we do, but it's made of this weird springy, spongy material and its eyes are like nothing I've ever seen before. Its eyes would give you nightmares for a month. And Dad had the cheek to say it was modelled on me. I hate it. Dad doesn't realize that he's created a monster. It's got to go. Watch this space.
Your friend, Claire.

I sat in front of the screen for a good ten minutes but Gail didn't reply. For the first time I wished I had more than just her e-mail address. I needed to talk to someone, really talk to someone who would understand how I felt. I had no doubt that Gail would sympathize with the way Dad treated me. All the time I'd been looking at the AI-2, it was as if it was pulling Dad further and further away from me. I lay on my bed, staring up at the ceiling. My PC was still on and set to alert me the moment I received an incoming mail message. I had some serious thinking to do.

When my PC bleeped, I leapt off the bed.

```
To: Claire@clairemail.private.uk
From: Gail@gailmail.private.uk

Dear Claire,
What're you going to do? Please
don't do anything too hasty. I'm
sure your father's new invention
means you no harm. Why don't you
try to get to know it first before
making up your mind to hate it?
I know it's OK for me to talk
because I'm not in your situation
but I'm sure your dad loves you
and would do anything to make you
happy. I really think you don't
know how lucky you are. I would
give ANYTHING to be in your shoes.
If I had one wish in the world it
would be that I could get away
from my father. I've never told
that to anyone but you. But I know
I can trust you. Please be
```

```
careful. You're a great pen pal
and I don't want to lose you. .
Take care. Your friend, Gail
```

My fingers flew across the keyboard after I'd read
Gail's message. I couldn't believe it. Of all people, she
was on Dad's side. Then I remembered something. I
went back over the messages she'd sent me. There it
was. I wondered why I hadn't picked up on it before. I
deleted the message I'd begun and started again.

```
To: Gail@gailmail.private.uk
From: Claire@clairemail.private.uk

Dear Gail,
You keep saying that you wish you
were in my shoes, but I don't
think you really understand what
I'm going through. You can't, or
you wouldn't wish that. You said
in one of your earlier e-mails
that your dad hopes you'll make
him rich one day. How are you
meant to do that? Do you have some
special talent then? If you have,
you kept that quiet! Your dad must
be a monster for you to envy me.
Can't you just leave and go and
live with other relatives? I'm
sorry I didn't ask before, I guess
```

I got caught up in what my dad was
up to. But believe me, my dad
really is horrible. He doesn't
care about Mum and me. We're just
two of his fans as far as he's
concerned. I'm going to change all
that. You just see if I don't.
Love, Claire.

But when I clicked on the 'Send' option at the top of the screen, I didn't know what I was going to do. I only knew I had to do something. I had to show Dad he couldn't treat Mum and me like this. So what could I do that would make him sit up and take notice of us? I leaned back in my chair and sighed. The only thing Dad had eyes for at the moment was AI-2.

So why not do something about AI-2 . . .

The thought entered my head, closely followed by a plan. If Mum couldn't do it, then I would. I would make Dad realize just how lucky he was to have his family.

To: Claire@clairemail.private.uk
From: Gail@gailmail.private.uk

Dear Claire,
Please, *please* think before you do
anything you'll regret. Claire,

you're worrying me. What are you
going to do? If you really won't
change your mind, then maybe I can
help you? After all, that's what
friends are for. I think - I
hope - I live close enough to you
to be of some help. Let me know
what you have in mind.
Your friend,
Gail.

I smiled when I read Gail's message and started
typing.

To: Gail@gailmail.private.uk
From: Claire@clairemail.private.uk

Dear Gail,
Thanks for your last message but I
think I can do this alone. Don't
worry. Let's put it this way: I'm
going to teach Dad a lesson.
Tonight, once Mum's asleep, I'm
going to phone for a cab and go to
Dad's lab and I'm going to sort
out the AI-2. Dad will be at the
lab tonight but even he isn't in
his office all the time. I'm going
to get rid of the AI-2. It's not
made of the same material as us so

```
it shouldn't be too difficult. I
don't know how Dad can say it's
more advanced than us when it's
made of something so soft and
squidgy. Its processor might be
advanced but what good is that
when its casing is so delicate?
I'm going to see just how delicate
it is tonight. Wish me luck.
Your friend, Claire.
```

I switched off the PC after that. I didn't want Gail to try and talk me out of it. I had to do this. It was the AI-2 or me.

I glanced down at my watch. Eleven-thirty. I shook my head as I looked up at Dad's lab. There was no turning back now, even if I wanted to – which I didn't. Mum had shut down for the night but if I went back home, she'd instantly reactivate. I didn't want that to happen. Not if I didn't have anything to show for it.

I walked around the back of the building and used Dad's spare keys to let myself in. The building was dark and quiet. I knew the two security guards would be at the front of the building, watching TV. I also knew that between eleven and midnight, Dad always wrote his daily journal down in the Abletech library which was two floors below his lab. So I had half an hour – or twenty minutes if I wanted to be on the safe side. I ran up five flights of stairs rather than take the lift and used Dad's keys again to let myself into his lab. I forced myself not to think about what I was doing. I forced myself not to think about the months and years Dad had spent working on AI-2. It came down to a simple choice. Dad's invention or Dad's family.

It was so bright, every light in the place must've been on, but it was eerily quiet. I looked around. The place was empty. I glanced down at my watch. I didn't want to get this wrong. Fifteen minutes left . . .

I crept across the floor to the adjacent lab. That had to be where Dad kept AI-2. She'd come out of that lab when Mum and I had first seen her. I opened the lab door – and gasped. The last time I'd seen this lab, it'd been full of tables covered with electronic devices and gadgetry. Now it was like someone's bedroom. There was a single bed against the far wall and opposite that was a table with a PC on it. The PC was switched on and I could see that it was connected up to the Cybanet.

'Hello, Claire.'

My head whipped round. There stood AI-2 watching me. It smiled and its whole face crinkled and wrinkled up. I couldn't help it. I took a hasty step backwards.

'I've been waiting for you.'

'What're you talking about?' My eyes narrowed. This thing was obviously trying to psyche me out.

'You couldn't possibly know I was coming.'

'You told me.' AI-2 smiled.

At my look of scorn, the AI-2 pointed to the PC screen across the room.

'Look for yourself if you don't believe me.'

Telling myself I was a fool to even glance in that direction, I sidled over to the screen, keeping a wary eye on the AI-2 before me. To my astonishment, I saw the last message I'd sent to Gail.

'What . . . How did you get that message? That was sent to my friend, not you. How dare you . . .?'

'You sent it to *me.*'

'Yeah, right! Since when is your name Gail and . . . when did . . . ?' I trailed off, staring at AI-2.

'Gordon's Artificial Intelligence Lifeform − or Gail for short,' said the AI-2.

'I . . . I don't believe it . . .'

'I told you not to do anything hasty.' The AI-2 started walking towards me.

I stumbled backwards. 'What're you going to do?'

'Talk to you. Reason with you,' the AI-2 replied.

I didn't take my eyes off the thing. I didn't realize I was backing away until I backed into the far wall opposite the door, jarring my body in the process. AI-2 stood directly in front of me.

'Touch me. Go on. Touch my hand,' the AI-2 ordered.

I tried to put my hands behind my back but AI-2 pulled them forward and placed my hands against its own.

'I know my covering isn't made of metal like yours, but does that really make me so repugnant?' AI-2 asked. 'I wish I did have a metal covering instead of this . . . this organic skin but that's how Father made me.'

'Father?'

'Your dad is my dad. He made me. I'm a carbon-based life form and my brain works by sending chemical as well as electronic signals. I have something called "blood" running through my body because I'm organic and the organs inside my body need oxygen to survive. The blood takes oxygen around my body and helps my body to repair itself and fight off any infections that might enter it. I work a different way from you but I still feel and think – just as you do.'

I stopped trying to pull my hand away from hers. Her skin felt so strange – warm and pliable. I looked down at my own hand. Grey-coloured jointed metal gleamed back at me.

'Father has come up with a new name for me,' said Gail. 'He calls me a "Humanoid". The next stage in the computer revolution. I can think and analyse just like you can, but I can also dream – something you Mechanoids have never been able to do. And I can adapt my own programming to create, by using something abstract called an "imagination".'

'And I suppose you think it makes you better than us Mechanoids?' I scowled.

'No, just different.'

'Why didn't you tell me who you were over the Cybanet?' I asked. 'Why did you lie?'

'I didn't lie. Your father calls me AI-2. I made up the name Gail for myself. And I do think of us as sisters. After all, at the very moment I became aware, I was *you*. After that moment, when I began to think and feel for myself, that's when my thoughts and feelings truly became my own. Up until then, they'd been yours.'

I watched Gail. She watched me.

'Your DNA? Where'd it come from?' I asked.

'I've spent the last few weeks finding that out for myself.' Gail sighed. 'I hacked into the government's computer suite and found some top-secret files. It seems that several thousand years ago there were quite a few life forms like me. We invented you Mechanoids but then a deadly virus killed off all the Humanoids and only the Mechanoids were left. I guess, because you had to fend for yourselves, you became self-aware and sentient. But you didn't want it known that you were *made*, so the information was kept secret and it's been that way ever since.'

'*You* made *us*?' I couldn't believe it.

'I have no reason to lie about it,' Gail said, her voice sad. 'Now do you see why I envy you? You have a mother and father and friends who are all like you. I call

Gordon "Father", but he never was and we both know it. Claire, everywhere you look, there are others who mirror your existence. But look at me. I'm thousands of years too late – or thousands of years too early. Either way, I'm alone.'

And for the first time, I began to wonder what it must be like to be Gail.

'Are you still going to destroy me? If you want to, I'll let you. You're the first one who's treated me like a real person rather than an experiment, but now that you know what I really am . . .'

'I was going to lock you in and burn this place,' I admitted. 'I only came in here to make sure that Dad hadn't taken you down to the library with him. You weren't a person to me, you were just a thing. I thought if Dad didn't have you any more, then maybe he'd come back to Mum and me.'

'And now?'

And that was the question. What was I going to do now?

It was in all the papers. They all wrote stories about the tragic loss of Gordon Drayton's lab and research data. Gordon Drayton, or Mechanoid 45902-X45-TAG4039, had the sympathy of the world. And it wasn't just the loss of all his research materials, but the loss of the AI-2 prototype which had everyone particularly dismayed. Dad and his colleagues tried to find bits of the AI-2 unit to at least have something to salvage, but because the AI-2 was an organic creature rather than metal, there was no trace of it left – that's what they all reckoned. And without Dad's notes, he was back to square one. I think the fire destroyed something in Dad as well, because after that, all his enthusiasm for his work just faded. He'd been knocked back too far to start again. I don't think he could face yet more years of research and analysis on historical DNA fragments before he'd ever have anything like the AI-2 again.

Mum said it was a real shame that the AI-2 died before Dad could show the world just what he had achieved. I didn't mean for Dad to stop working. I didn't want him to come back to Mum and me that way. Gail and I just wanted it to look as if Gail had been destroyed in the blaze. At first I was very upset about Dad, but I found that the sadness I felt diminished with each passing day. This time next year, I don't expect to feel anything at all. Mum and Dad were right. My feelings are disappearing. I think I'm growing up at last.

I only *feel* about two things now. One is Gail. The other is the thought of imprinting my synaptic patterns on an infant Mechanoid unit. I look forward to having my own child. I'll do a better job than my dad did with me. I won't love it or anything like that – I'm no longer capable of such emotions, but I know I'll feel something.

And I'm glad. I wouldn't like to lose feelings entirely –
although no doubt one day that's exactly what will
happen.

```
CLAIRE DRAYTON - MECHANOID 39028-
X46-TAG4054

PERSONAL LOG: DATE:8 FEBRUARY 7504
AD

I've got Gail hidden where no-one
will find her. We removed as many
of Dad's disks containing his
research notes as we could and
I've promised Gail that I'll do my
best to follow in Dad's footsteps
when I get older. Gail doesn't
want to be the only one of her
kind anywhere in the world. It
would be great to create more
Humanoids like Gail. Dad was right
about that at least. Her processor
is equal to mine and then some. I
enjoy listening to her talk. Some
of the things she talks about -
like the pattern of the clouds and
dreams - can only make me wonder,
and envy her. She can actually
make up stories on the spur of the
moment which have no basis in
truth whatsoever. It seems to come
```

as naturally to her as breathing.
I find I'm beginning to understand
Dad's obsession with her.

As for Gail, every time she
hears about Dad sitting at home,
just staring at the walls, the
strangest thing happens. Her face
gets very wet. I think it's called
– crying.

She may be the smartest computer
in the world, but she has
feelings. And from the look of it,
unlike with us Mechanoids, her
feelings are never going to pass.
She'll never grow out of them.
I'll have to see if I can make the
next Humanoid without permanent
feelings. Privately I can't help
thinking that it doesn't matter
how clever or creative their
processors (or as Gail calls them,
their 'brains') are, if they never
grow out of their feelings,
ultimately they are bound to fail.

AMAZING ADVENTURE STORIES
Collected by Tony Bradman

I almost laughed out loud. Except that pistol was wavering all over the room. Then it suddenly went off . . .

Ever wondered what you would do if you came face to face with a Nazi parachutist in the Second World War, or were held hostage in the middle of nowhere for your dad's riches? What if you were marooned on a desert island on your way to Australia? Or caught up with a murderess?

Tony Bradman has collected ten action-packed adventure stories from a team of top authors such as Malorie Blackman, Robert Westall, Douglas Hill and Helen Dunmore in this fast-moving and gripping anthology. Your nerves will never be the same again!

'Excitement, fear and suspense in equal measure . . . all the stories are thoroughly entertaining'
School Librarian

0 552 52768 8